Worzel Gummidge

When Susan and John see the scarecrow standing in the middle of a field in the pouring rain, he doesn't look that remarkable. Just like any other scarecrow really. But when he turns up at the cottage to warm himself by the fire, they realize that this is a very special scarecrow indeed.

The scarecrow's name is Worzel Gummidge, and together he, John, and Susan embark on a series of wonderful adventures.

Barbara Euphan Todd was born in Yorkshire and began to write when she was only eight years old. It was, of course, some years later that Worzel Gummidge made his first appearance in 1936. He quickly became a firm favourite and reached an even wider audience when his adventures were broadcast in his own television series.

Worzel Gummidge

Barbara Euphan Todd

Illustrated by Tony Ross

OXFORD
UNIVERSITY PRESS

Dedicated gratefully to
HUGH E. WRIGHT
who played the part of Worzel Gummidge so
successfully in the Regional Programmes at
Broadcasting House

OXFORD
UNIVERSITY PRESS

Great Clarendon Street, Oxford OX2 6DP

Oxford University Press is a department of the University of Oxford.
It furthers the University's objective of excellence in research, scholarship,
and education by publishing worldwide in

Oxford New York
Athens Auckland Bangkok Bogotá Buenos Aires Cape Town
Chennai Dar es Salaam Delhi Florence Hong Kong Istanbul Karachi
Kolkata Kuala Lumpur Madrid Melbourne Mexico City Mumbai Nairobi
Paris São Paulo Shanghai Singapore Taipei Tokyo Toronto Warsaw

with associated companies in Berlin Ibadan

Oxford is a registered trade mark of Oxford University Press
in the UK and in certain other countries

First published 1936
First published in this paperback edition 2002

Database right Oxford University Press (maker)

British Library Cataloguing in Publication Data available

ISBN 978 0 19 275102 7

3 5 7 9 10 8 6 4

Typeset by AFS Image Setters Ltd, Glasgow

Printed in Great Britain by
CPI Group (UK) Ltd, Croydon, CR0 4YY

Paper used in the production of this book is a natural, recyclable
product made from wood grown in sustainable forests. The manufacturing
process conforms to the environmental regulations of the country of
origin.

Chapter 1

Probably if it had not been for whooping-cough, John and Susan would never have seen the scarecrow who stood in the middle of Ten-acre field.

They had been sent down to the country at a time when the place was all muddy and slushy, almost empty of flowers and very full of lambs. All the excitement of being ill—meals in bed, blackcurrant jelly, and unexpected presents—was over, and nothing remained except what Emily Goodenough called 'the tag end of a cough'. Emily had been their nurse, but now she lived with her sister who was married to a farmer in Scatterbrook, and she always invited the children down to the village for part of the summer holidays. They enjoyed those visits when even the farm kitchen smelled of hay and clover and honey, and when the tortoiseshell cat basked on the wall until his fur was as hot as sun-baked bricks, but the country was disappointing in early spring.

Whooping-cough had left them cross and quarrelsome. They weren't allowed to go near other children because they were still infectious, and all the grown-up people of the place were too busy to be bothered with them. They couldn't spend much time in the lofts because the dry hay-dust got into their throats and made them cough. They weren't allowed to play in the farm kitchen except on soaking days, because Emily said, 'Fresh air is the best doctor.' So every morning, after breakfast, they were bundled into overcoats and mufflers and wellington boots, and told to go for a nice brisk walk and to keep out of mischief and to turn their heads away and try not to cough if they happened to meet any other children.

At first it had been rather fun, but after they had walked as far as they could in every direction, and had explored most of the ditches and hedges, and found some new and a lot of old birds' nests, they began to get rather tired of everything and particularly of each other.

John said he didn't want to have to go for walks every day with a girl of twelve who thought she knew everything, and Susan said she didn't want to have to go for walks with a boy of ten who didn't know anything at all.

One morning when they were in the middle, or perhaps it may have been nearly at the end of a particularly long quarrel, they came to a gap in a hedge, and decided to go through it because they were tired of the road.

'We'd better not!' said Susan, as a tiresome bramble tugged at her coat. 'We'd better not go across the field. There's a man in the middle of it, and he's waving his arms at us.'

'That's not a man!' said John when he had peeped over the hedge. 'That's a scarecrow.'

'It's a man. I saw him pointing at us, and then he waved his arms about. We'd better go back.'

'Let's look!' said John, and he pushed his way through the gap in the hedge, and past Susan.

When he had looked, he laughed in the sort of way he always did when Susan was making as much room for cows as was possible in a narrow lane, or when she was walking very, very quickly past the farmyard geese.

'That's a scarecrow,' said John, 'and if you're

frightened of it, you must be a crow. Scared crow! Scared crow! Scared crow!'

'I'm not a crow and I'm not scared!' Susan pulled her coat away from the bramble, and followed John into the field. 'But he did move. I saw him. He stood still as soon as you looked at him. Now he's begun again. Look!'

The children stood quite still, and stared at the figure in the middle of the field. It was a good long way away from them, so they could not see it very distinctly, but they saw that it was dressed in an old black coat and long trousers, and that its hat was tilted on to the back of its head. Its arms were stuck straight out from its shoulders.

While they waited, the rain began to fall, slowly at first, and then very fast indeed.

'We'd better shelter under the hedge,' said Susan.

John answered crossly, 'There's *no* shelter under that silly little bit of hedge. We'd better take a short-cut across the field.'

'It may be a long-cut. We don't know the way.'

'It can't be a long-cut. The road's a long-cut: it's so winding. Wait till I get my compass out.' John began to unbutton his overcoat, and got very wet indeed as he was doing it, because he forgot to turn his back to the rain.

By the time the compass had been dropped

several times in the mud, Susan didn't particularly mind which way she went home, and she felt sure that even the most angry man wouldn't be more angry, even if they did take a short-cut across a private field.

So John had his way, and they began to run as quickly as possible over the deeply ploughed furrows. They could scarcely see the creature in the middle of the field because the rain was beating down so heavily.

Their wellington boots stuck between the furrows so often that it took quite a long time to cross even a quarter of the field.

Once or twice Susan said she was quite sure that she had seen the man coming towards them, but John, who was shorter in the leg and shorter in the wind than she was, seemed too breathless to answer.

At last, when they had very nearly reached the middle of the field, one of John's boots came right off, and they had to wait for some time, because when he tried to push his foot into it again the boot sank deeper and deeper into the sticky soil, and when he stood on one leg and pulled, he tumbled over. By this time they were standing almost opposite to the scarecrow, and Susan saw that he had a most friendly and pleasant face. It was cut out of a turnip, and one or two green leaves stuck out from under his black bowler hat.

'Oh!' cried Susan, 'he's got an umbrella. He's holding it in his, his—' She looked more closely, and saw that the scarecrow hadn't got a hand. The round, polished end of a broom-handle showed beyond his ragged cuff. 'It's sticking out from his *arm*!' she ended.

'Let's take it,' said John. 'My neck's as wet as anything and *muddy*.'

He looked almost as much of a scarecrow as the scarecrow itself, for he had fallen down twice, and all one side of him was plastered with wet earth.

'I don't think we ought to take the umbrella,' said Susan.

'Why not?'

'It belongs to him.'

'It's not a he; it's an *it*!'

'S'sh!' said Susan, for somehow, though she could see that the scarecrow's face was made out of a turnip and that his nose was just a knobble and his mouth only a slit, he looked as though he might come to life any moment.

'Let's see if the umbrella works,' said John, and he gave another tug at his boot, and then walked towards the scarecrow.

And then, just as he was nearly in reach of the

broomstick arm, something whirred past his head.

'Ooh!' said Susan.

'A robin!' shouted John. 'It came out of the scarecrow's pocket. There must be a nest in it. Look, I can see the bits of hay and stuff sticking out of his pocket.'

'Don't touch it,' said Susan. 'Don't touch it. Robins desert if you touch their eggs. Emily told me. There's a rhyme about it—

"'"The robin and the red-breast, the robin and
    the wren,
If you take out of their nests you'll never
    thrive agen!"'

'All right!' replied John. 'We won't touch, but we'll look.'

Both children walked right up to the scarecrow. John had to stand on tiptoe before he could peep down into the tiny nest of the breast pocket of the coat, but the top of Susan's head was nearly on a level with the scarecrow's round, turnipy chin.

'Four eggs!' said John. 'P'raps there'll be another one tomorrow.'

Susan stepped closer to the scarecrow and as she did so, she trod on something that was quite stiff and crunchy.

'Oh! I'm sorry!' she said.

'What's the matter?' asked John.

'I trod on his foot,' explained Susan. 'I trod on his straw boot.'

John looked down at the bottle straws that stuck out from each of the scarecrow's trouser legs.

'Those aren't boots,' he said. 'They're the things that bottles are packed in. Come on. Let's go home. I'm simply sopping.'

He lifted the umbrella from the scarecrow's stiff arm, and began to put it up. It wasn't much of an umbrella, but it was better than nothing even though two of its ribs were quite bare, and though there were jagged holes in the stuff that covered the rest of it. The wind tried to tug it out of John's hand, and the rain beat fiercely down on to the shabby, green silk.

'I don't think you *ought* to take it,' protested Susan. 'It belongs to him.'

She looked up into the scarecrow's face as she spoke, and was glad to see that he was still grinning. The rain had washed his face almost clean, and several drops were trickling down his face. He looked like someone who was unhappy, but trying to be cheerful.

'He's crying,' said Susan. 'He doesn't want us to take his umbrella. P'raps he puts it up at night when nobody's looking.' John grasped the umbrella more firmly, and walked away.

'He doesn't deserve to have an umbrella if he doesn't use it in this rain. Besides, he's only a scarecrow.'

By this time Susan felt so very cold and wet that she turned to follow John.

'We'll bring it back in the morning,' she said.

'Ooh aye!'

'What did you say?'

'I didn't speak,' answered John, who was trying to prevent the umbrella from turning inside out.

'You did!'

'I didn't!'

'Someone did.' Susan sounded rather frightened, for she had an uncomfortable feeling that the scarecrow must have spoken.

She turned round several times to look at him, but he seemed to be standing quite still. Susan felt rather glad that his back was turned to them. When she looked for the last time, she saw that the robin had returned, and was preening herself on the top of the bowler hat.

The children had a long, uncomfortable walk home. The umbrella behaved as badly as umbrellas always do when the wind is blowing. Little trickles of rain ran down its rusty ribs, and rain spurted through the big holes and ran down Susan's neck, and John's arm. Presently she took the umbrella, and soon her sleeve was dripping wet too.

Some of the rain found its way into the tops of the wellington boots, so that after a time the children's feet made squelchy noises with every step they took.

Long before they reached the end of the field, Susan and John were so breathless that they began to cough rather badly. Every time they coughed, they whooped.

'That's the danger signal again,' said Susan. 'That shows we're still infectious.'

Emily Goodenough had told them that whoops were danger signals, and that until they had not coughed in that uncomfortable way for at least a week, it would not be safe for them to play with other children.

'Can't help it,' said John, and he whooped again, rather more loudly than he need have done, because he was proud of the noise he made.

'Let's hurry!' gasped Susan. 'We mustn't catch cold or Emily will be in a rage.'

But it wasn't easy to hurry, even when they left the field and began to walk down the muddy lane that led to the village. Their clothes were heavy with rain, and they seemed to be carrying pounds of mud on each boot. Susan didn't mind the walk so much as John did, for she had an excited feeling inside, though she didn't know why.

At last they reached Mrs Kibbins's cottage that stood at the end of the village street, and presently they passed the red house where Mrs Bloomsbury-Barton lived. She was the one person in the place who didn't seem to belong to it. She wore London clothes even in the morning, and on Sundays she wore kid gloves and high-heeled shoes and a hat with a great many bows on it. The children generally met her on days when they were particularly messy and untidy, and she always looked at them in such a way that they felt as though their faces were growing dirtier and dirtier and the holes in their stockings bigger and bigger.

'She won't be out today,' panted John. 'That's one good thing.'

Five minutes later, they were slushing through the mud of Mr Braithewaite's farmyard, and ten minutes after that they were standing in their dressing-gowns by the kitchen fire while Emily scolded, and rubbed their hair, and told Mrs Braithewaite to hurry up with the blackcurrant tea. It was all very warm and comforting.

Chapter 2

That evening, John was sent to bed early because he was rather shivery and because he had whooped six times running, but Susan was allowed to sit up, and have her bread and milk by the fire.

It was very still in the room, but every now and then the silence was disturbed by some comforting country sound: there was the rattle and splosh of Susan's spoon as she dipped it in and out of the bread and milk, the click of Mrs Braithewaite's knitting needles, and the whistling noise of Farmer Braithewaite's pipe. Then the kettle began a little bubbling sound, and the tortoiseshell cat, not to be outdone, yawned, stretched herself, and purred a tune that rhymed with the bubbling. And all the time the wind rattled the windows.

Susan jiggled her spoon, and thought about things. She was careful not to make a noise, for that might remind Mrs Braithewaite that it was long past bed-time. Emily had gone to a social in the village, and her sister had promised to look after the children. Mrs Braithewaite was a thin, rather fussy little woman; she wasn't at all like the pictures of farmers' wives in any book that Susan had ever seen. *They* were always fat, pleasant-looking people, but Mrs Braithewaite had a face that was rather like an angry weasel's. She had red hair, too, just the colour of a weasel's, and she had pale blue eyes. All the same, she was generally quite nice.

Mr Braithewaite looked exactly like a farmer; he was red and fair and fat, and he wore leggings that smelled of oil, and breeches that were too tough to be torn by any bramble. Mr Braithewaite began all his sentences with 'HEY!' and he talked a great deal about the weather. He had lived in Scatterbrook all his life, but he did not seem to know very much about it, though Susan had asked him a lot of questions. She was sure that

13

there was something magic about the place even in the wintertime.

It was not that Scatterbrook looked particularly different from all the other villages that struggled up the hillsides, or huddled their red roofs together in the green lap of the downs. The golden weather-cock on Scatterbrook's spire was no brighter than the burnished bird on Dimden's steeple. The stream that wound its tinkling way through Penfold and stirred the rushes in the Fairfield meadows ran no more joyously over the stepping-stones in Scatterbrook. Perhaps it even hushed its tumultuous jubilation just a little when it had passed the mill, but that may have been because it was nearing the sea, and so dreamed a little fearfully of the grey, hedgeless furrows that were soon to take the place of the friendly plough-lands.

Susan found it difficult not to believe that most things were alive. She thought the windows of houses were eyes, and she was particularly fond of cottages in Scatterbrook because they nearly all had thatched eyebrows. She felt quite certain too, that the scarecrow must be alive, or very nearly.

As she was thinking about him the latch of the door rattled, then dropped, and then rattled again.

Farmer Braithewaite, who had been drowsing over his pipe, woke with a jerk, glanced at the clock, stood up, and said, 'Hey! I'll go up to the lambing pens now, and see if the shepherd's wanting any help.'

When he had finished speaking, Susan heard a rustling movement outside the window and, after the farmer had opened the door, a sharp scent of turnips drifted into the room.

'I'll make the barn ready,' said Mrs Braithewaite, 'in case you bring some lambs back with you.' For once, she forgot Susan; lambs in Scatterbrook were more important than little girls. And for once Susan didn't beg the farmer to take her with him. She had the sense to know that if she spoke she would be noticed, and that if she were noticed she would be sent to bed.

When the farmer and his wife had left the kitchen, the latch rattled again.

The tortoiseshell cat stopped washing her ears, and glanced over her shoulder. Then the door opened very slowly, and a strange-looking visitor shambled into the kitchen.

Susan recognized him almost at once.

'Evenin'!' said the scarecrow and Susan wondered where she had heard his voice before. He stared round the room, then he coughed as sheep do on misty autumn nights. Presently he said, 'Evenin'!' again.

'Good evening!' said Susan politely.

'You needn't be scared,' he told her. 'It's only me!'

'I'm not scared. Only just at first, before I remembered. I thought you might be a tramp.'

'Not me!' he replied. 'I'm a stand still, that's what I am. I've been standing still, rain and fine, day in and day out, roots down and roots up.'

He began to walk crab-wise across the kitchen; one arm was stretched out sideways, and the other one was crooked at the elbow. As he walked, his bottle-straw boots made scratching noises on the stone floor.

'You'll wonder what I've come for!' he said.

But Susan didn't particularly wonder, for it seemed perfectly natural for him to be there. She stared at him, and decided that his straw boots could not be really comfortable for walking in.

'I've come to save you a journey,' said the scarecrow. 'At least, partly to save you a journey and partly to save myself from missing it.'

'From missing what?' asked Susan.

'The umbrella. Where is it?'

Susan was so astonished that she could only point to the row of pegs on the door. The farmer's coat hung on one, and Mrs Braithewaite's

16

overall was on another. The third peg held a cap and the scarecrow's umbrella, or what was left of it.

'I'm so sorry,' said Susan at last, 'but you didn't seem to be using it and so—'

'I know all about that,' replied the scarecrow. 'I heard you argufying.'

'If we'd known you could talk, we'd have asked you to lend us the umbrella,' explained Susan. 'I did think though that I heard you speak, just as we were going away.'

'That's right. But I'm not much of a talker except now and again.'

The scarecrow took his umbrella down from the peg, and stroked it once or twice. Then he dropped it with a clatter.

'I might as well sit down,' he said, and moved towards the fireplace. 'How do you?'

'Very well, thank you,' said Susan politely, though she couldn't think why he was asking the question *then*.

The scarecrow looked puzzled. 'I mean,' he explained, 'I mean how do I sit? Is it difficult the first time you do it?'

But Susan couldn't remember, for she was so very used to sitting. She continued to look at the scarecrow. His face certainly was remarkably like a turnip, and yet his widely-grinning mouth had a kindly expression. As he waited, the lump in the middle of his face began to look quite like a real nose. Just as Susan was wondering what to say next, he lifted the little hen robin from his pocket, and gently rubbed his cheek with her wing feathers. 'It's still a bit damp outside,' he explained, as he popped the bird back into its place. 'I always use her as a handkychiff.'

Then he suddenly moved backwards, lifted both feet together and sat down on the hearth-rug with his legs sticking straight out in front of him.

So that's how they sit, thought Susan.

The tortoiseshell cat looked very offended, and stalked out into the scullery.

The robin fluttered back into his pocket and began to make rustling noises inside it. Susan remembered then that the scarecrow in Ten-acre field had had a robin's nest in its breast pocket. Just as she was wondering if there was a father robin, another little bird suddenly hopped out from his hiding-place under the scarecrow's widely-brimmed hat, looked round importantly, straddled his legs, jerked his tail. Then, encouraged by the reflection of the fire gleaming on the sunny surface of a warming-pan, he began a mad little song.

Susan leaned forward and touched the scarecrow

on the knee. She longed to be friendly with anybody who kept robins in a coat pocket.

'What's your name?' she asked.

'Gummidge,' he replied. 'I'm Worzel Gummidge. I chose the name this morning. My granfer's name was Bogle.'

'Gummidge isn't a very pretty name,' objected Susan.

'No,' he replied. 'It's as ugly as I am.'

Susan looked at him. His hat was awry over his turnipy face. A shabby black coat hung from his shoulders, and one arm was still akimbo. But she noticed that he had managed to bend his knees a little, and that his fingers, which two minutes before had looked like bits of stick, were more human now; they even showed lumps that might possibly be mistaken for knuckles. He was growing less like a scarecrow every minute. Soon, thought Susan, he might look more like a man than Farmer Braithewaite.

'Gummidge isn't pretty,' she said, 'but it's a very interesting name.'

'Ooh aye!' he agreed. 'But then, I've a power of things to interest me—roots tickling and shooting, rooks lifting in the wind, rabbits here, there, and scattered in a minute. Give over now, do!' This last remark was made to the cock robin, who was pecking at his greenly-bearded chin.

'How old are you?' asked Susan.

'All manner of ages,' replied the scarecrow. 'My face is one age, and my feet are another, and my arms are the oldest of all.'

'How very, very queer,' said Susan.

' 'Tis usual with scarecrows,' replied Gummidge. 'And it's a good way too. I get a lot of birthdays, one for my face and another for my middle and another for my hands, and so on.'

'But do you get presents?'

'Well, I haven't had many so far,' confessed Gummidge, 'but then I've seldom thought about having birthdays. *Will* you give over!' He raised a hand and pushed the little bird back again under the shadow of his hat.

'Do you often walk about?' asked Susan.

'Never done it before!' declared Gummidge. 'But I says to myself last night, when I was standing in Ten-acre field, I says to myself, "You ought to go about the world and see things, same as the rabbits do. What's the use of having smart legs," I said, "if you don't use them!" ' Gummidge stroked his shabby trousers proudly. 'I says to myself, "You might as well be rooted for all the travelling you do." So this evening, after the rooks had stopped acting silly, I pulled up my feet and walked about a bit. Then I went up to the sheep pens and had a bit of a talk with one of the ewes.'

'Which one?' asked Susan.

'Eliza, her that has the black face,' replied Gummidge. 'But she was a bit short with me; she was so taken up with her son and daughter.'

'Has she got lambs?' asked Susan.

'Ooh aye! She's got a black son and a white daughter. She says they're the finest lambs in Scatterbrook and that they're wearing the best tails *she's* ever seen. I said to her, I said, "You needn't talk; there's a hazel bush at the corner of Ten-acre which is fair covered with lamb's tails, and she doesn't make such a song about it." After that the ewe turned her back on me.'

'Why did you come here?' asked Susan.

'Well, I had thought about going to London instead,' replied the scarecrow. 'I thought I'd go to London, till I met a mouse in the lane and she changed my mind for me.'

'Why did she?'

'She had been to London herself. She was a fieldmouse, and she'd heard tell of stowaways. So she stowed herself away in a market basket and she saw Piccadilly.'

'Did she like it?' asked Susan.

'Well, I don't know about that,' replied Gummidge. 'But she saw a policeman, and he was dressed just the same as the one in Scatterbrook, and she said if they couldn't do better than that in

Piccadilly, she'd come home again. And she said they told such lies. There's a place they call St Martin in the Fields, and it isn't in the fields at all. There's another place called Shepherd's Market, and she said there wasn't a shepherd there. So she said London was all a sham and that it was trying to copy Scatterbrook, so she came home again. And I've come here to fetch my umbrella.'

'Are you going to stay in Scatterbrook?' asked Susan eagerly. She had taken a fancy to Worzel Gummidge and she hoped that he'd teach her how to talk to sheep and how to tame robins.

'I might,' said Gummidge carelessly. He raised a hand and lifted a piece of mud from the place where his right ear should have been. Susan saw that his fingers moved stiffly as scissors and that his thumbs were like sticks. Then his head drooped forward and he fell asleep again.

The crackling of the fire, the singing of the kettle, and the soft powdery shuffle of falling ashes blended themselves into a jumble of sound, and Susan too fell asleep.

When she awoke, morning had slipped unnoticed into her bedroom, and she remembered having been tucked into bed very late indeed, because Mrs Braithewaite had forgotten all about her, and because Emily had not returned until eleven o'clock.

She was so sleepy that it was not until she was halfway through her breakfast, and John had finished eating the islands in his porridge that she remembered anything at all about Worzel Gummidge.

'Had the scarecrow gone away when you came home, Emily?'

'The what?' asked Emily.

'Eat up your bread and marmalade, for goodness' sake do,' said Mrs Braithewaite. 'I must get cleared away if I'm to do anything this morning. We're late as it is.'

Susan sighed, for she knew it would be no use to ask any more questions while Mrs Braithewaite was in that sort of mood.

After breakfast she told John all about Worzel Gummidge, but he said she must have been dreaming, and that the scarecrow was still in the field.

'How do you know where he is?' asked Susan.

'I saw him before breakfast. I went out to look at that robin's nest, but I didn't get far enough. The scarecrow was there, though.'

'Oh look!' said Susan. 'He's forgotten his umbrella.' She pointed to the pegs on the kitchen door. The old umbrella was hanging from one of them.

'That proves he didn't come at all,' said John in his most provoking voice.

If it hadn't been for the lambs, Susan herself might have thought that the scarecrow's visit was only a dream. But when Farmer Braithewaite came into the kitchen, and said, 'Hey! What do you think the ewe with the black face has got?' Susan knew the answer.

'I know! I know!' she cried. 'She's got a black son and a white daughter, and they're wearing the best tails she's ever seen!'

'Well, I never! Who's been telling you that?' asked the farmer.

'Gummidge,' said Susan.

'Gummidge?' The farmer looked puzzled. 'There's nobody of the name of Gummidge hereabouts.'

Susan was saved from answering because Mrs Braithewaite called, 'George, George! There's a strange cat slinking round the chicken coops.' So away went the farmer, leaving Susan to triumph over John.

'What did I say! What did I say! What did I say!' she shouted, and as if she hadn't said enough to prove that Worzel Gummidge really had paid a visit to the farm, a tiny brown feather fluttered down from the kitchen mantelpiece.

'That belongs to the robin!' said Susan.

Chapter 3

Presently Susan forgot all about Worzel Gummidge, for the sun came out and shone so brightly that Emily said the children had better have a picnic up on the top of the Beacon Hill. A picnic in spring is really an adventure.

For half an hour Emily bustled about, until her round cheeks were quite flushed and her hair rather untidy. She ladled hot stew from Mrs Braithewaite's casserole jar, and put it into two jam-jars. She buttered newly baked bread, and made strawberry jam sandwiches, and then she filled a bottle half full of milk and half full of cream. Then, when the jars and bottles had been wrapped in hay and put into an old carpet bag, Mr Braithewaite brought the dog-cart round to the front door, and said that he would drive the children to the bottom of Beacon Hill. John filled his pockets with string, and Susan took both her penknives, a card of darning wool, and two shoe-boxes, for Emily had told them that the Beacon woods were yellow with primroses, and they had decided to send presents to all their friends.

They had been to the place before, but only in the summertime when all the birds' nests were empty and untidy, and the leaves were so thick that you could scarcely see the branches of the trees.

They reached the top of the hill by eleven o'clock, and then they had lunch because they simply couldn't wait for it any longer.

After they had hidden the jam-jars in a hollow tree, had given some sandwich to a friendly chaffinch, and had tried to tame some very young rabbits, they began to gather primroses.

The flowers were growing in thick clumps underneath the beech trees, and there were so many of them that even when the children had picked twelve bunches there seemed to be as many on the ground as before. Susan's hands were as cold and pink as primrose stalks by the time she had finished picking, and the tip of John's nose was quite damp because he had stopped to smell the flowers so often.

Susan didn't remember Gummidge again, until she passed the top of Ten-acre field on the way home.

'He must have gone for a long walk,' she said, as she pointed to the empty field. 'I hope he won't need his umbrella.'

'I expect Mr Braithewaite's moved him to another field,' said John.

Just then a little cock-robin flipped over the hedge.

'Wife! Wife! Wife!' he scolded.

'There, you see!' cried Susan. 'Gummidge *has* gone for a walk, and he's taken the nest and Mrs Robin with him. I do think he might be more careful.'

But John wasn't listening to Susan; he was staring down the lane. Some way in front of them walked Mrs Bloomsbury-Barton. By her side, keeping pace with her mincing steps, was Worzel Gummidge. He was moving sideways, and so of course he was looking straight into her face.

'That's Gummidge!' cried Susan.

'It can't be!' said John, but he sounded rather doubtful all the same, for the scarecrow's clothes were not the sort that could be forgotten in a hurry. The children could see that Mrs Bloomsbury-Barton was agitated by the way the feathers on her hat bobbed about. She walked slowly, and so did Gummidge. She quickened her stride, and so did Gummidge. She stood still, and so did Gummidge.

Susan could scarcely believe what she was seeing. John laughed. 'Some tramp has stolen the clothes off that old scarecrow,' he said.

The robin, who was still circling above the children's heads, uttered a fierce cry of 'Wife! Wife! Wife!' and went zipping along between the hedges. He landed with a jerk of his tail on to Mrs Bloomsbury-Barton's hat, swayed disgustedly on a tuft of feathers, and then flew across to Gummidge's shoulder.

Mrs Bloomsbury-Barton turned aside, and began to walk towards a gap in the hedge, but Gummidge followed her. By this time the children were near enough to hear what was being said.

' 'Tain't fair!' said Gummidge. 'Other folks did ought to take their turns!'

'You forget yourself!' snapped Mrs Bloomsbury-Barton.

'Not me!' said Gummidge. 'Now listen here,

missus—all I wants is for you to take a turn at scaring while I walks about a bit. It should be easy for you with those whiskety feathers in your bonnet!'

'I don't know what you're talking about!' Mrs Bloomsbury-Barton shook her umbrella in a threatening way.

'Fine!' shouted Gummidge encouragingly. 'You just keep on trying, and you'll make a fine scarecrow. Why, you might have been brought up to it!'

'Good morning!' said Susan. She noticed that the scarecrow looked much more like a man than he had the night before. Though his face was rather rough and knobbly, it was not so very like a turnip. He seemed to have grown fingers, and his mouth moved more easily.

'Good morning, Susan,' said Mrs Bloomsbury-Barton in a reproving voice. 'Good morning, John. You children had better come home with me.' She lowered her voice, 'I have been having a good deal of trouble with this tramp. He is a most objectionable man, and has followed me all down the lane.'

'He isn't exactly a tramp, you know,' said Susan. 'He's—'

'Don't argue, dear,' said Mrs Bloomsbury-Barton. 'Come along, John.'

She began to hurry down the lane again, and the children followed rather dismally.

'I'll come too,' remarked Gummidge to Susan. 'This bird and I—' He waved a stiff arm towards Mrs Bloomsbury-Barton and one of his stick-like fingers scraped against the silk of her umbrella.

'She isn't a bird,' whispered Susan, though she could scarcely speak for laughing. As a matter of fact, at that moment, Mrs Bloomsbury-Barton did look rather like an angry turkey. Her face and neck were quite red with temper.

'Maybe she's not a bird *yet*!' Here Gummidge pulled gently at one of the plumes in the lady's hat. 'She may not be a bird yet, but she's having a real good try. Some be slow fledgers!'

'Don't answer him,' said Mrs Bloomsbury-Barton. 'Don't speak to him. The man must be quite mad!'

Once more Gummidge tweaked at a feather, and Mrs Bloomsbury-Barton tossed her head so haughtily that her hat came off in the scarecrow's hand.

'Moulting!' he said sorrowfully, and he bent his earthy head over the hat.

'That's queer now! Not many birds moult before they've finished fledging, not even rooks, and they're queer enough.'

'Come away!' said Mrs Bloomsbury-Barton to

the children. 'Come away! I shall go straight to the policeman, and ask him to put this man under restraint!'

'You might lend me your umbrella!' coaxed Gummidge, stretching out his hand towards the ivory handle.

But Mrs Bloomsbury-Barton could not bear it any longer. She forgot the children. She forgot her dignity, and she forgot her hat. Gathering her rustly skirts above her plump knees, she almost ran down the lane that led to the village.

Gummidge looked after her sadly. 'What a waste of a fine scarecrow,' he muttered. Then he sat down on a heap of stones and began to take the hat to pieces.

'It'd make a good nest,' he said, turning it upside-down.

'I don't think you ought to do that,' said Susan in her primmest voice. All the same, she was delighted to see the wreck of Mrs Bloomsbury-Barton's hat, for its owner was not a nice person.

'I think he *ought*,' said John suddenly. It was the first time he had spoken since the children had met the scarecrow.

Gummidge looked up and grinned. 'Me and your sister gets on nicely together,' he remarked. Then he began to tear a feather into shreds, muttering, 'She loves me, she loves me not,' all the time he was doing it. It took him quite a long time to reach the end of the feather. John crept closer to watch, but as the scarecrow seemed much too busy to take any notice of him, he pulled Susan aside, and began to whisper to her.

'Do you think he really is a scarecrow?'

'I know he is,' said Susan firmly.

'Then we'll be able to have fun with him. We can play with him. He won't catch whooping-cough.'

'She loves me not,' wailed Gummidge as he tore away the last little bit of feather, and flicked it over towards the robin. 'It does seem a pity.'

'Who doesn't love you?' asked Susan.

'That bird that said she wasn't a bird.' Gummidge sniffed miserably, and the children saw that his face was covered with moisture that might have been dew and might have been tears, though it didn't look quite like either.

'She's a horrid old thing,' said John consolingly. 'She wants to teach everyone how to behave.'

'Just what I want to know!' said Gummidge, and, snatching Father Robin from his shoulder, he wiped his damp face with the bird's wing. 'I was thinking how nicely we might have got on together, her in the field and me out of it. Me in it and her out of it. I'd have seen a bit of life and she'd have seen a bit of field.'

'We'll show you,' said John.

'Show me what?' asked Gummidge.

'We'll show you how to play with us.'

'But you're not full-growed,' sighed Gummidge. Just then a loud bellow sounded behind them, and a dun-coloured cow put her head over the fence. Susan backed away rather nervously, but Gummidge rose stiffly to his broom-sticky legs, and, stretching out an arm, scratched the cow between the horns.

'Mrs Bloomsbury-Barton's coming back!' shouted John. 'I can see her head bobbing along round the corner.'

'She maybe changed her mind,' said Gummidge, and a pleased smile stretched over his face. 'To think she's never seen my lovely shirt.'

He jerked himself out of his coat, and hung it on a hedge stake. Then he sat down stiffly, and, tweaking another feather from the hat, he began a second game of 'She loves me, she loves me not.'

John wondered why he was so proud of his shirt. It was very tattered, and was faded to the mottled blue of a house-sparrow's egg. As for his braces, they were simply strands of tarred string knotted together.

'You had better run away,' said Susan to

Gummidge. 'Mrs Bloomsbury-Barton's bringing the policeman with her.'

The scarecrow didn't answer, but he dropped the hat, and sat quite still.

A strange procession was coming down the lane. It was headed by Mrs Bloomsbury-Barton and the village policeman. Behind them came the milkman, two farm labourers, the village postmistress, and several children.

'Do go!' whispered Susan.

'You'll be put in prison if you don't,' said John. The scarecrow sat so still that the children found it difficult to believe he had ever moved. His legs were stuck out stiffly in front of him, and his face looked very turnipy.

Nearer and nearer came Mrs Bloomsbury-Barton and the village crowd.

The dun-coloured cow mooed disconsolately and so loudly that Susan and John felt perfectly certain that she too was asking Gummidge to run away. And then, when the policeman was within a few yards of him, and Mrs Bloomsbury-Barton had begun to point with her tightly-gloved finger, Gummidge spoke to the cow. Neither of the children could hear the words, but Susan declared afterwards that the cow must have understood for she nodded, or anyway lowered her horns. Then Gummidge sat down on the ground again.

'There he is!' shouted Mrs Bloomsbury-Barton, and she pointed her finger at Gummidge, from the place where she stood.

Then something very amazing happened. Susan always said that Gummidge must have had something to do with it. The dun-coloured cow charged through the hedge, and, lowering her horns, she ran straight for Mrs Bloomsbury-Barton. Now, ordinarily she was a placid enough cow. John had often rubbed the knobbly ridge between her horns; and even Susan in a brave moment had once laid her cheek against the dun-coloured cheek and caught whiffs of the sweet, milky breath. But now the cow seemed to have gone mad. She kicked her heels and ran through the crowd. She arched her back and then straightened it in sudden jerks, as though her spine was made of giant catapult elastic.

Mrs Bloomsbury-Barton scrambled for the opposite hedge. The cow just stopped to thrust a horn through the hat on the ground, and then charged after her, frisking her tail and lowering her head.

The policeman and the postmistress and the milkman and the labourers and the children all joined in the chase. And right across the fields scooted Mrs Bloomsbury-Barton, her petticoats flying in the wind.

John and Susan stood on the gate and watched. They saw Mrs Bloomsbury-Barton scramble over a distant gate, and then they saw the cow, who was still wearing the hat on her left horn, turn aside and begin to eat grass. She looked as though she had never chased anyone in the whole of her peaceful life.

'I believe Gummidge told the cow to chase people,' said Susan.

'Rot!' said John, and then as all the other people in the field began to follow Mrs Bloomsbury-Barton, he jumped down from the gate and ran towards Gummidge.

The scarecrow was lying on his back by the side of the road. His eyes were closed; at least if he had ever had any eyes they were closed. His fingers appeared to be simply pieces of twig, and the space between his trousers and bottle-straw boots showed two round and polished broom-handles. Gummidge had turned himself back into a scarecrow.

'Now you see,' said Susan triumphantly. 'He is a scarecrow. Why! Whatever has happened to his nose?'

'He hasn't got one,' said John.

It was perfectly true; there was only a little earthy knobble in the middle of a very old turnip. It was round and it bulged, but it wasn't a nose.

There wasn't a mouth either, nor a chin nor eyes; there were only a few odd hacks and scratches— a gash for a mouth and two scratches for eyes. The scarecrow had the kind of face that any child might have drawn on a slate and labelled 'This is a man!'

'It's very queer,' said John. 'Do you think the tramp was a magician?'

'Of course he wasn't a magician,' said Susan. 'He was never a tramp at all. He was just a scarecrow who came alive. Now he's gone dead again, just as I was getting fond of him!' And she burst into tears.

'Hush,' said John. 'Somebody is coming back.'

The policeman's helmet appeared over the top of the hedge. He climbed over the gate and a little boy followed him. Susan and John were just in time to slip behind the hedge.

'He's gone, Mister,' said the little boy. 'No, he hasn't; he's there, see!' and he pointed a grimy finger towards Gummidge.

The policeman stepped across the road.

'That's only an old scarecrow!' he said. But he looked rather puzzled and, stooping over Gummidge, he raised one broomstick arm. There was a horrid sound of tearing sacking, and the straw rustled huskily.

'Coo!' said the little boy. 'That's Farmer

Braithewaite's scarecrow out of Ten-acre field. How did it get here, Mister?'

'How should I know?' said the policeman. 'We can't do with old rubbish littering up the roadside.'

He stooped down and hoisted Gummidge on to his shoulder.

John and Susan, who were peeping through the hedge, held their breath as they saw Gummidge's head droop waggishly sideways, and loll against the policeman's shoulder.

'Coo!' said the little boy. 'He's all stuffed with straw.'

'Here goes!' grunted the policeman, and he heaved Gummidge over the hedge.

'Good riddance to bad rubbish,' said the postmistress. The scarecrow nearly fell on the heads of John and Susan, who were crouching beside a bramble bush. He landed on the ground with a limp plop.

'Coo!' said the little boy, and then he and all the other people followed the policeman down the road.

Chapter 4

John look at Susan and Susan looked at John, but neither of them spoke. The truth was they felt a little shy of one another after the queer thing that had happened. Magic is ordinary enough in a book, but it seems a queer thing in real life. They felt rather lonely and miserable, as though a party had stopped in the middle, and left them alone with a Christmas tree whose candles have been blown out.

They had just begun to get used to the scarecrow's queer ways and knobbly face. He was such a nice sort of betwixt and between person, not quite grown up though he seemed as old as the fields, and yet not quite a child either, though in some ways he seemed as young as they were.

They admired him too, for having dared to make fun of Mrs Bloomsbury-Barton, a thing they had wanted to do ever since they had seen her important walk and fussy clothes.

Then, too, they had wanted to ask Gummidge the sort of questions that no ordinary person could answer; questions about rabbits and robins and crows. And now, here he was lying at their feet, and looking as lifeless as a sawdust doll that has lost most of its stuffing.

'I'm afraid he's dead,' said Susan, as she glanced down at the turnip face.

'Perhaps he's only pretending,' said John.

'He may only have been *pretending* to be alive!' said Susan. They sat still and thought about this for quite a long time, but it was all so muddling that at last they had to stop.

'If he had stayed alive,' said Susan at last, 'if he had stayed alive, or even if he had only *pretended* to be alive, I think he would have been a very great friend of ours. He would have been such fun at parties.'

'And I'm sure he would have had a very good way with mud,' added John.

Then Susan continued: 'He'd have been the

very person to take exploring with us; we could have sent him through the hedges first, and it wouldn't have mattered about his clothes.'

A big bluebottle fly buzzed out of the hedge and settled on the knobbly lump in the middle of the turnip face. Just for a moment Susan thought that the scarecrow twitched his green eyebrows; but decided that she must have been mistaken, for though she stared at him for quite ten seconds, he did not stir.

She took out her handkerchief, and flapped at the fly, who buzzed angrily away to be pounced on by Father Robin, who had returned to the coat in the hedge, so as to see how his wife was getting on.

'It must be tea-time now,' said John. 'We had better go; Mrs Braithewaite will be cross if we are late; besides we don't want any grown-ups to ask *reasons*.'

'But we'll come back the second afterwards,' said Susan. She said it rather loudly, so that Gummidge should hear, just in case he were pretending to be an ordinary scarecrow. She rather hoped that if they went away, Gummidge would follow them; she felt perfectly certain that no scarecrow could go on lying by the side of the road; she had never seen one do such a thing before.

It seemed rather a long way back to the village. The road was sticky and troublesome, and the picnic bag scratched the children's legs. Everything seemed very dull and uninteresting. Just as they reached Mrs Bloomsbury-Barton's horrid-looking red house, Susan stopped. She sniffed, and then fumbled in the pocket of her jersey.

'Bother! I've left my handkerchief behind,' she said.

'Use mine,' said John.

'No thanks. Besides, it's a rather important birthday-present handkerchief. We must go back.'

It didn't take them long to reach the gap in the hedge. They knew it was the right place, because Gummidge's coat was still hanging in the hedge. Father Robin was singing a little song from the topmost spray of a hawthorn tree. They stopped to listen, and suddenly they were startled by a very peculiar sound from the other side of the hedge; it sounded like a muffled motor-horn, and it ended in a splutter. They heard a sniff, then another splutter and the odd, honking noise. They crept quietly through the hedge and, as they did this, they heard a sudden movement on the grass. Gummidge was still flat on his back, but by his side, crumpled into a tight ball, lay Susan's handkerchief.

'He has been using it!' she cried. 'It was all neatly folded up. And now it's scrunched and rumpled. Look!'

'Cheek!' said John.

They waited for some moments, but nothing happened.

'We'll go away and leave him,' said John loudly; he put his finger to his lips and beckoned to Susan to follow him back on to the road.

'Listen,' he whispered. 'If Gummidge has used your handkerchief, he must have a nose, mustn't he? *If* he has grown a nose again, he must be turning into a real person. So let's keep very still and watch.'

They lay flat on the roadside and peered through the hedge.

Presently Gummidge's right foot stirred a little; then his left one moved. He sat up stiffly and looked cautiously about him. His face was still turnipy, but wasn't quite so knobbly as it had been. He seemed to move with difficulty; rather as though he had been frozen and was slowly thawing. Presently he stretched out an arm, stuck one finger under Susan's handkerchief, and, very, very slowly closed his thumb over it. He used his hand as though it were a stiff pair of scissors. Then he bent forward, covered his face with the handkerchief and once again the children heard the peculiar honking sound that scarecrows make when they blow their noses.

By the time he had dropped the handkerchief his face looked almost human, though his expression was rather cross. Father Robin hopped down on to his hat, but the scarecrow knocked him off angrily. Fumbling in his pockets, he produced a broken clay pipe. He stuffed this full of grass, and began to suck it furiously.

'Gummidge!' called John.

Gummidge took no notice at all.

'Worzel Gummidge,' whispered Susan, but the scarecrow continued to suck at his pipe. Even when the children came through the gap in the hedge and said, 'Won't you talk to us?' he continued to stare moodily up at the sky.

'I believe he is offended with us,' said Susan to John, as she stooped down and stroked Gummidge's shirt sleeve. He shook himself angrily.

'What's the matter?' she asked.

'Leave me be,' he replied. 'I'm sulking!'

'But people don't say when they are sulking; they just sulk,' objected Susan.

'I'm not people. I'm one scarecrow. You've asked and I've told you,' snapped Gummidge. 'Sometimes I sulks for hours and sometimes I sulks for weeks; it's in the family, we're all the same.'

'But it's very, very horrid to sulk,' said Susan.

'It's perfectly beastly!' said John.

'It hurts nobody,' said Gummidge. 'My old nurse often says it hurts nobody; she should know, being a fitful body herself, and having reared many children.'

Gummidge didn't look at all the sort of person to have a nurse. Susan decided that she must be a very careless one, since his ears were so shockingly muddy.

'Have you still got a nurse?' asked John in amazement. 'Have you still got a nurse—a great scarecrow of your age?'

'Leave me be,' said Gummidge. 'Leave me be, and let me have my sulk out.'

He lay back on the grass and pouted. The turnip skin stretched tighter and tighter and tighter. Every little wrinkle and dent was smoothed out, until the dried mud from all of them trickled in grey powder down Gummidge's face. He looked terribly sulky.

'Do tell us about your nurse,' begged Susan; but he only pouted more furiously than ever, while the dust rained down his face.

Then Mrs Robin, who had been popping her head in and out of her nest, scrambled out on to the lapel of his coat, and whisked up and down on his shoulder. For some time she pecked insistently at his muddy ear, and chirruped plaintively.

Quite suddenly Gummidge smiled; the turnip skin relaxed into its usual pleasant furrows. He wiped the loosened mud from his green beard, smoothed the robin's feathers rather jerkily, and said, 'Ooh aye, my dear; be off and enjoy yourself!'

'Do you mean us?' asked Susan.

'No,' replied Gummidge. 'It's the robin's afternoon off.'

The little bird, in answer to a petulant cry from her husband of 'Wife! Wife!' flipped over the hedge and away across the meadow.

'Won't the eggs get cold?' asked Susan.

'Not in here, they won't,' replied Gummidge: he crooked stiff fingers and pulled the nest out of his pocket; then, very very carefully, he tucked it inside his patched shirt. 'One of my odd jobs,' he remarked.

'It seems a very odd job,' agreed John. 'I suppose you *are* quite sure that they won't hatch out into baby scarecrows.'

'Sure as sure!' replied Gummidge. Then he turned to Susan and asked, 'How long did I sulk for, that time?'

'For about five minutes, I should think.'

'Not long enough,' said Gummidge, and he began to stiffen again.

'Oh! please don't,' begged John.

'Well, I've had enough to annoy me,' said Gummidge. 'But I don't mind if I don't.'

'Tell us about when you were little,' begged John, and Susan added: 'I'm sure you must have been a very dear little scarecrow.'

'I never was little,' declared Gummidge indignantly. 'Nor were Granfer Bogle neither!' and he looked angry again.

'Well, tell us how you began,' said John.

'I didn't begin; I was put together in a mortal hurry. 'Tis the same with all of us. We stays the size we're made; and we're made to fit our clothes.'

'Why?' asked John.

' 'Tis only sense. Your sort are made backwards way on.'

'We aren't,' said Susan.

'Now listen here,' said Gummidge, and the children, seeing that he was in a talkative mood, settled themselves on the grass.

'Now, see here,' continued Gummidge. 'Your clothes are made to fit you, and you wears a lot on 'em. Well I wears a lot on 'em too. I've a shirt and a weskit and a pair of string braces, and a hat and a pair o' bottle boots. Now if I'd 'a' been made *first*, then the clothes mightn't have fitted so fine; but, seeing as I was made to suit the suit, I didn't give much trouble, did I?'

'No,' said Susan. 'But then what will happen when your clothes wear out!'

'They was wore out, long afore I had 'em,' explained Gummidge proudly. 'The trousers was wore out by the squire, the coat was wore out by the vicar, the boots was wore out by the bottles, and the string was muddied already. The more wore out clothes is, the better for scaring rooks; the creatures are so tidy themselves, except about the nest.'

'But who made you?' asked John.

'Nobody in particular,' said Gummidge. 'My face was carved out of a turnip by a chap who came hedging and ditching. He just took a clasp knife and hacked away. Then some other folks brought the broom-handles and a bit of straw. They soon had me set up and into the sacking. And then they put my clothes on. I was a lovely fit, so my old nurse tells me. I was a grand fit until the spadgers came.' Here Gummidge sighed deeply, and patted the robin's nest.

'What did the sparrows do!' asked Susan.

'They stole my stummick,' sighed Gummidge sadly.

'How horrid of them!' said Susan with a shudder. 'How very, very horrid of them; so rude too. What did they want it for!'

'To make their pesky nests with. There was a

hole in the sacking, an' a weskit button was off; an' they nipped out my straw stuffing to make their nests with—shocking bad nests too, and that extravagant—'

Once more Gummidge's face was covered with the unhappy moisture that Susan had noticed before. He felt on his hat for Father Robin, found he was not there, so he fumbled for Susan's handkerchief and wiped his face proudly.

'Go on,' begged John. 'Do tell us some more. How did you come alive?'

'So far as I can mind,' said Gummidge slowly, 'so far as I can mind, it all started with a itching in the head, when the turnip began to sprout. Then there was a tickling on the chin, where the beard was growing; after that I couldn't stop myself.'

'But what I don't understand,' said Susan, 'what I don't understand is how do you turn yourself from a scarecrow into a person?'

'Aah!' replied Gummidge. 'That would be telling, that would.'

'Do tell,' begged Susan.

John said scornfully: 'I don't believe he knows himself.'

'I don't,' agreed Gummidge. 'Your sort turns into men, but you don't know how you does it. Eggs turns to chickens; apples turns to dumplings; milk turns to cheese. None of them knows how they does it, leastways they don't say so! It's a changeable world.'

'But they don't chop and change as often as you do,' said Susan.

'Water turns to ice and ice turns back again to water, when it's had enough of itself.'

'It doesn't change as quickly as you do,' argued John.

'Maybe it's not so impatient. I'm a terrible hasty fellow and *that* inquisitive. Well, I must get to my rook-scarin' now.' He rose stiffly to his feet, and began moving sideways to the gate.

'Do you know the time?' asked John.

'It's the wrong season for dandelions,' said Gummidge.

Susan thought that he must have gone mad; then she remembered that a scarecrow would be likely to tell the time by dandelion clocks.

'But they tell a different time, whenever you blow; don't you find them muddling?' she asked.

'Time always is different,' said Gummidge. 'All the time it goes on being different. Good day to you. I'm going to have a real good sulk in Ten-acre. See you in the morning.' Then he edged away, and though the children called after him repeatedly he would not so much as turn his head.

They were very late for tea, and Mrs

Braithewaite was cross. She had been doing a heavy day's baking, and the kitchen was full of the smell of dough and freshly-baked loaves. Farmer Braithewaite had not returned from the market, and as Emily had gone with him, there was no one to welcome the children.

Susan and John went into the orchard and played at being the Swiss Family Robinson until Mrs Braithewaite called them in to supper.

Chapter 5

John awakened early the next morning, and, jumping out of bed, he rushed across to the window. Far below him, the little stream twisted in and out of the mottled patchwork of the valley. The golden weather-cock gleamed on the church steeple, and the roofs of the cottages were all newly washed and shining with rain. But John didn't notice any of these things. He gazed across the fields to where Gummidge, looking like a very untidy crow, was waving raggedy arms at the rooks.

Susan was awake too; she lay in her bed and

listened to the jingle and clang of the milk cans in the yard below, and wondered if Gummidge could come to see them or if they would be able to go and see Gummidge. She thought it would be better for the scarecrow not to come to the farm too often. Probably, Emily would not think he was a fit sort of person for them to play with. Emily had a lot of queer ideas about properly brought up children.

After breakfast, Mr Braithewaite asked John if he would go to Pendleton and buy a copy of *Exchange and Mart* from the station bookstall.

'A very good idea!' said Mrs Braithewaite. 'That'll keep them quiet and give Emily and me a chance to do the dairy work!'

John and Susan did not think it was at all a good idea, but they couldn't possibly explain that they would rather not go to Penfold because they wanted to play with a scarecrow.

They did not get back until eleven o'clock. As they returned through the village street, they noticed that all the old ladies, who lived in the thatched cottages, were leaning over walls, chattering and gossiping. Even the most friendly of them only nodded hastily to Susan and John.

When they reached the farm, they pushed the newspaper in through the parlour window; then they made their way round to the kitchen door.

Mrs Briggs, the village washerwoman, was sitting in the rocking chair, swinging herself violently backwards and forwards. Her shining face, which always looked as though it had been carved out of a piece of common, yellow soap, looked very agitated. She twisted her pink, shrivelled fingers together, and spoke in short jerks.

'I wouldn't mind so much if it wasn't for Mrs Bloomsbury-Barton's new chemises.'

'Now don't take on so, my dear,' said Mrs Braithewaite. 'You let me make you a nice cup of tea and then tell us what has happened.'

The washerwoman stopped rocking herself for a moment, and gulped, 'I wouldn't mind so much if it wasn't for Mrs Bloomsbury-Barton's chemises; she is such a very particular lady.'

'What's the matter?' asked Susan, and John echoed, 'What's the matter?'

Nobody took the slightest notice of the children.

'I wouldn't mind so much if it wasn't for the squire's vests!' She rocked about again, this time so violently that she nearly upset the chair. 'All trimmed with lace they were.'

'You don't say!' cried Mrs Braithewaite. 'You'd never guess it to look at him; and him such a nice, quiet gentleman and so fond of his cat. Does he have lace on his *shirts*?'

'It's Mrs Bloomsbury-Barton's chemises that have lace on them; that's what I'm so worried about, and it's a lovely drying day.'

Mrs Braithewaite, who was bustling about the kitchen, preparing a cup of tea, stopped and said, 'Now just you tell me all about it.'

The washerwoman gulped. 'It's a beautiful drying morning. Mrs Bloomsbury-Barton's chemises looked a treat and so did the squire's vests and the policeman's pyjamas. I'd washed them beautiful and set them on the line. Aye, but it's Mrs Bloomsbury-Barton I'm so worried about.' Here she flung her apron over her head and sniffed loudly.

'Here's a nice cup of tea,' said Mrs Braithewaite, as she uncovered the washerwoman's face and passed her a steaming cup.

'I'd hung all the washing out, and I'd gone into the house to make myself a nice cup o' tea, the same as I always do, when I saw a shadow pass the window. It made me come over all queer. But I said to myself, "Now just you have a nice cup of tea, and rest your poor arms; it's a beautiful drying morning." So I had my cup of tea. Then it came on to rain, so I went out to the green to take in the clothes. Oh, deary me today! Oh, deary me today!'

Once more the washerwoman broke down,

and Susan noticed that her face looked like soft soap—all jellified and quivering.

'Go on!' said Mrs Braithewaite.

'The washing was gone!' moaned Mrs Briggs. 'The washing was gone and the line was as—as bare as my arm, save for the children's little bits of things.'

'You don't say!' said Mrs Braithewaite.

The washer-woman nodded dismally. 'Such a beautiful drying morning, too. Who could have taken them? That's what I want to know.'

'Maybe someone has been having a game with you,' suggested Mrs Braithewaite.

'Mrs Bloomsbury-Barton will have a game with me when she hears of it. She'll have a game and all; and her without her chemises.'

'What sort of a game?' asked John with interest. Neither the washerwoman nor Mrs Bloomsbury-Barton had ever struck him as being in the very least playful.

'Maybe a tramp took them,' said Mrs Braithewaite.

'What about Gummidge?' whispered John to Susan.

'Well, I'd best be moving,' said the washerwoman. 'I'll go and tell the policeman, not that he's much use at finding things.'

She gave herself a final rock, and walked across

the kitchen. When she reached the door, she turned and said, 'I wouldn't mind so much if it wasn't for Mrs Bloomsbury-Barton's new chemises.'

'I think we had better go and look for Gummidge,' said Susan, as soon as the washerwoman was out of sight.

John nodded solemnly.

But when they reached Ten-acre field, the scarecrow had vanished. He was not in the next field, nor in the spinney, nor down by the water-meadows. They hunted in all the places they could think of. At last Susan suggested that they had better return by Ten-acre field, just in case Gummidge had only been for a short walk.

As they were crossing a corner of the field, Susan noticed something black and raggedy hanging in the hedge.

'Gummidge's coat!' she cried. 'Perhaps he has gone to sleep in the ditch.'

But though they made quite sure that the coat was Gummidge's because of the robin's nest in the pocket, there was no sign of the scarecrow himself.

Susan asked the robin where Gummidge had gone, but of course the little bird did not answer; she only stared at Susan out of her impertinent little black eyes. She looked as though she were keeping the most important secret in the world.

'Perhaps Gummidge has run away to sea,' suggested John. 'Or he may have gone out into the world in search of his fortune. I'm afraid he must have left Scatterbrook for ever.'

'It's rather noble of him to leave his coat for the robin, isn't it?' said Susan. 'Perhaps he is descended from Sir Walter Raleigh.'

They hunted about for a little longer; then they decided to go home.

The washerwoman was leaning over her gate as they went through the village. Half a dozen of her friends were gathered around her. The children heard her raise her querulous voice as she said: 'I wouldn't mind so much if it weren't for Mrs Bloomsbury-Barton's chemises.'

So they knew that the washing had not been found, and they wondered if Gummidge could have taken it.

'He looks very honest, though,' said John.

'But then he may have been badly brought up. If you are sort of dragged up in a hurry and then put straight away into other people's clothes, it must be rather difficult to know what does belong to you,' said Susan.

After they had finished lunch, Susan and John went into the orchard again. It was a good place to play in, with all its twisted old trees. Just as they were wondering whether the big apple tree in the far corner should be a house or a ship, they heard the sound of tearing calico. An enormously fat woman was climbing over the hedge. She looked like a giant plum pudding on legs. Her head was too small for her huge body, and she wore a sunbonnet that nearly covered her face. She balanced for a second on the top of the hedge; then she caught her foot, tumbled over and rolled towards the children.

'Whoever can she be?' asked Susan, looking timidly at the shapeless mass on the ground. The woman was certainly dressed very oddly. She appeared to be wound about with sheets, and she grasped a string of knotted handkerchiefs. This was so long that it had not finished following her over the hedge. She revolved rapidly for some seconds. When she stopped, John, who had excellent manners, said, 'I do hope you haven't hurt yourself.'

The white bundle wriggled violently. Then she sat up and coughed. The sunbonnet still covered her face, and her hands were entangled in the folds of her clothing.

'Can I help you?' asked John.

'Ooh aye!' said a familiar voice. There was another jerk of the sunbonnet, and the knobbly face of Gummidge beamed up at the children.

'Oh!' said Susan. 'Then it was you all the time.'

'O' course it were!' said Gummidge.

'*You* took the washing off the clothes line,' said John.

'Who else?' asked Gummidge pleasantly. ''Twere quite easy. Why shouldn't I take my turn? Other folks had worn the clothes all the week. I wanted to give the rooks a good scare. And I did too.' Here he broke off, and chuckled wheezily.

'But, it's very, very naughty of you,' said Susan. 'The poor washerwoman was so worried about Mrs Bloomsbury-Barton's chemises.'

Gummidge looked terribly sulky, as he answered, 'I don't want the pesky things. I've kept on stepping on them wherever I've trod.'

'Then they'll be muddy,' said Susan.

'Sure to be,' agreed the scarecrow. 'Now do give me a bit o' help.' He rolled over on his back, and lay there with his legs and arms sticking up stiffly in the air. Susan thought that he looked just like a large and helpless beetle, but he smiled up at her so engagingly that she simply could not feel angry with him.

'Come on, let's unroll him,' said John.

The two of them seized the outside sheet, and began to tug at it.

Even then it took quite a long time to get the sheets off Gummidge. They were twisted in the most amazing manner, and were terribly muddy. Mrs Bloomsbury-Barton's chemises were knotted together and tied sashwise round an enormous pair of pink pyjamas. Underneath the pyjamas was a nightdress; underneath the nightdress was a pink flannel petticoat; underneath the petticoat was a blue overall, and underneath that was Gummidge's own waistcoat.

The scarecrow was not in the very least helpful. He did not attempt to bend his arms or legs. But Susan, who was quite good at undressing dolls, managed somehow or other to tug the clothes off the stiff limbs.

'That's better,' said Gummidge. 'That's quite a deal better!' Suddenly he bellowed, rather in the manner of a sick cow. John had stuck a safety pin into the back of his neck.

'Do be quiet,' begged Susan. 'Anyone might think you were killed!'

'Anyone might think right, too!' roared Gummidge. ''Tain't safe to go jerking about any longer. I'm going to have a real good sulk.'

'Oh, don't!' pleaded Susan. But it was too late. Already Gummidge's features had melted into the turnip of his face. His limbs were rigid, and there was a rustle of straw as John tugged at the blue overall.

'It's perfectly beastly of him,' grumbled John. 'He might *try* to help. Now I suppose he'll sulk for hours!' Susan tried to help. She wrenched Gummidge's arm out of the overall, and began to unwrap the bath-towel that was twisted round his legs.

'It's worse than undressing a jointless doll,' she said.

The children worked so hard that they did not hear the sound of footsteps close behind them.

The first thing they heard was Emily Goodenough's voice.

'I wouldn't have believed it of you,' she said. Susan and John raised their untidy heads, and saw a row of angry faces peeping at them from over the orchard hedge.

Mr and Mrs Braithewaite, the washerwoman, and Emily must have heard Gummidge's shrieks.

'I wouldn't have believed it,' repeated Emily, and the washerwoman wailed, 'I wouldn't mind so much if it wasn't for Mrs Bloomsbury-Barton's chemises!'

Susan and John looked imploringly at Gummidge. He lay on his back with one torn bath-towel wrapped round his neck. His arms were stretched out straight on either side of him.

Wisps of straw stuck out from his cuffs. His face was muddy and knobbly. Altogether he looked the most raggedy scarecrow in the world.

'I couldn't have believed it,' said Emily. 'Now what have you got to say for yourselves?'

Neither Susan nor John had anything to say, for they knew Emily would never believe their story. They didn't feel they could blame her either, for they could scarcely believe the truth themselves.

'You see—' began Susan miserably.

'I see you've done the worst bit of mischief you ever *have* done in all your born days,' scolded Emily.

'It's the scarecrow!' said John.

'Anyone can see *that*!' roared the farmer. 'And who told you to take it out of my field, I should like to know?' John looked at Gummidge, and gently prodded him with his foot.

'Ask him,' he muttered.

'If you're going to be rude on the top of all this naughtiness—' threatened Emily.

Susan stooped down, and began to drag the bath-towel from Gummidge's neck.

'Leave that filthy thing alone,' scolded Emily, 'and come straight back to the house.'

Susan deliberately poked her finger into Gummidge's eye, but even that didn't make him move.

'We were trying to help,' she explained. 'We've been trying to help all the time. We took the clothes off him as quickly as ever we could, and *we* didn't get them muddy.'

'No!' agreed John. 'They, they sort of *got* muddy!' After that, everyone began to talk at once; that is, everyone except Gummidge. The washerwoman wailed about Mrs Bloomsbury-Barton's chemises. The farmer grumbled, Emily scolded, and Susan began to cry. And all the time, Worzel Gummidge lay on his back in a dead sulk.

Suddenly, Mrs Braithewaite began to be rather kind. She told Emily that children would be children.

'I wish scarecrows wouldn't be scarecrows,' muttered John, which was unwise of him.

'This one won't be a scarecrow for long,' said Farmer Braithewaite. 'I shall have him pitched on to the bonfire first thing tomorrow morning!' He climbed over the hedge and gave Gummidge a kick.

'You couldn't be so cruel!' sobbed Susan.

'Scarecrows aren't things for children to meddle with,' snapped Emily, and John felt inclined to agree.

'This one's about done for, anyway.'

As Farmer Braithewaite spoke, he picked

Gummidge up, and flung him over one shoulder. A melancholy procession returned to the farm. Emily announced that she would have to help the washerwoman to scrub the clothes and that it would take her half the night.

'We'll help, if you like,' said Susan. But of course the children weren't allowed to do anything so amusing. They were sent out for a dull walk, and told to keep to the roads and not to go near the village.

Before they went, they saw the farmer fling Gummidge into an empty stable, and turn the key in the door.

Chapter 6

Susan and John felt rather muddled the next morning. They were still angry with Gummidge for letting them be scolded for his tiresome adventure, but all the same they could not help feeling sorry for him. The stable where he had spent the night was such a dull, gloomy place.

After breakfast, when they went into the farmyard, a hen was clucking importantly to her family of chickens, whose down was as yellow as the primroses up on Beacon Hill. The tiny birds staggered out from under their mother's wings, balanced themselves on spindly legs, and peeped up at the children, as though to say, 'Who are you and what are you doing? Don't you know that the world began yesterday?'

'Let's go and peep through the stable window,' said Susan after she had finished playing with the chickens. 'Shall we go and ask Gummidge why he was so horrid yesterday?'

'No,' replied John. 'It's our turn to sulk now. Next time I see Gummidge, I shall pretend not to know him.'

'Perhaps we never shall see him again.' Susan's freckled face looked quite miserable.

'Well, I don't care. He's not at all a nice person. He's a beast!'

'Not exactly a beast,' said Susan. 'Not exactly a beast, but he's dreadfully uncomfortable to be friends with.'

Just then Emily came bustling into the yard, and asked the children to go to the vicarage, and find out what time the jumble sale would begin.

'What jumble sale?' asked Susan.

'What is a jumble sale?' asked John.

'Now run along do, there's good children, and don't stop to worry me with questions.'

Emily seemed to have forgotten her crossness of the day before, and the children thought they had better not remind her of it by arguing, so they hurried away.

'Gummidge's old coat would be a good sort of thing to take to a jumble sale,' remarked Susan as they turned into the lane. 'It's shabby enough for the very best sort of jumble sale.'

'Let's get it,' cried John, and they raced across a field where the corn was beginning to thrust its little green swords through the earth.

When they reached the place where Gummidge's coat, all silvery with dew, was hanging on a hedge-stake, they remembered that of course it couldn't be sold, because of the robin's nest.

'I'd rather like to wear it myself,' said John. 'I'd love to have a robin's nest in my pocket.'

'It's much too dirty,' objected Susan. 'Emily would say it's infectious.'

'Why? Gummidge isn't ill.'

'You might turn into a scarecrow if you wore his coat.' John made a face, and then turned to follow Susan down the lane that led to the vicarage.

They rang the doorbell as Mrs Parsons was saying to her husband, 'Do you think the squire's trousers are worth half a crown?'

Mrs Parsons was as brisk as her husband was dawdlesome, and as plump and perky as he was slow. She looked in a great hurry.

Susan repeated Emily's message, but Mrs Parsons didn't seem to be listening. She pointed to some wisps of straw that littered the hall, and said, 'Such a strange looking man came here this morning. He was begging for a coat. I told him that he had better come to the jumble sale this afternoon. But he said he hadn't any money. I said that we would pay him if he could cut the grass for us, but he said he couldn't do that until this evening. He was very queer. Just look at all those wisps of straw: he shook them out of his shirt-sleeves.'

Susan looked, and at once she was reminded of Worzel Gummidge. Surely nobody else would be so untidy.

'Do you think he could have been one of Farmer Braithewaite's men?' asked Mrs Parsons.

'No!' said John, because he didn't think that any of Farmer Braithewaite's men kept straw in their shirt-sleeves.

'Yes,' said Susan, because she knew that Gummidge belonged in a kind of a way to Farmer Braithewaite.

Mrs Parsons didn't notice their replies, though, because she had just discovered some bits of mud on a chair, and the children were able to slip away.

As they came home, through a small paddock

that opened on to the farmyard, they passed a great pile of rubbish that had been heaped ready for burning. It was very slushy and muddy in that corner of the paddock, and as they picked their way through the thick mud they were startled by a particularly violent sneeze.

'Gummidge!' whispered Susan. 'I'm sure it must be Gummidge.'

'Don't take any notice of him,' begged John, and he hurried on.

Susan simply couldn't help looking round. She saw Gummidge lying in a most uncomfortable position on the rubbish heap. His head was hanging down and his legs stuck helplessly in the air.

'Morning!' he wheezed.

'Come *on*!' said John, and he ran through the farmyard gate.

'Morning!' repeated Gummidge pathetically. 'I can't take off my hat; it's tumbled into a puddle.'

He looked so miserable that Susan couldn't help speaking to him.

'You *were* horrid not to tell Mrs Braithewaite that it was your fault about the washing,' she said reproachfully.

'I'm not much of a one for talking to strangers,' explained Gummidge modestly. 'I generally sulks when I'm spoken to suddenly. It's a form of shyness. You'd never believe how shy I am.'

He struggled violently, and presently he managed to sit up with his back to Susan.

'Why are you on this horrid old rubbish heap?' she asked.

'I've been thrown away!' said Gummidge sadly. 'I'm going to be burned this evening, so the farmer says.'

'How very, very horrid,' said Susan.

'Isn't it?' replied Gummidge cheerily. 'But then you see, it's in the family. They always burns one of my cousins every fifth of November. I remember saying to Guy one evening late in October: I says to him, "I'm glad it's you and not me." And he answered, "Well the nights are getting chilly, and anyway the fireworks will be a treat." That's what Guy said!'

'But are the Guy Fawkes *alive*?' asked Susan in horror. She had always enjoyed fireworks and bonfires.

'Well, they're alive on and off—the same as me. But they are subject to sulks, too, so they don't feel the fire. Still, I don't want to be burnt. It seems such a waste of my trousers, and I'd made such nice plans. I'd arranged to have the vicarage grass cut this evening. It does seem a pity. Ooh aye! It does seem a pity.'

'But why do you *stay* here?' asked Susan.

'I'm used to staying where I'm put,' replied Gummidge. He looked so forlorn, so tattered and muddled and helpless, that Susan splashed through a puddle and climbed up on to the rubbish heap beside him.

Then she began to talk to him in the way that she talked to dolls and puppies and babies. She wiped his muddy face with her handkerchief. She tried to pull his neck-band straight. She felt rather glad that John had left her alone with Gummidge. Presently she helped him to get up, and hand in hand she and Gummidge went across the fields together. Susan was determined that the scarecrow should not sit still and wait to be burnt.

They went into Ten-acre field, where Susan found his coat in the hedge and helped him into it, though Father Robin was very indignant.

Then, once more putting her hand into his knobbly one, she led him along the little winding lane to the spinney.

'I think you had better hide here for a bit,' she said. 'What are you going to eat for your dinner?'

'Oh, I dunno,' said Gummidge. 'I'll find something—bits of roots maybe. There's always some sort of food in the woods for those as takes the trouble to look for it. Maybe the squirrels will help me find a bit of something, and the birds might too.'

A dreadful thought came into Susan's mind. She hardly liked to mention it, and yet she felt that she must know.

'You don't,' she began, 'you don't eat *worms*, do you?'

'Certainly not,' said Gummidge, with dignity. 'I don't eat anything that doesn't keep still.'

Then Susan left him, for she didn't want to be late for her own dinner.

In the afternoon, John and Susan went to the vicarage jumble sale with Emily Goodenough, who seemed to have forgotten all about their whooping-cough.

Emily wanted to buy a hat that had been sent by Mrs Bloomsbury-Barton and the children wanted to buy anything that they would not, in the ordinary way, be allowed to have, so they took their pig money boxes with them.

When they reached the vicarage, they saw that the lawn was covered with stalls which were heaped with old clothes and the odds and ends from half a dozen attics.

All the old ladies from the almshouses were swooping down on hats and petticoats. They jerked their arms in and out of coat-sleeves. They jostled one another, flapping and chattering like the seagulls that follow the plough on windy March mornings.

Presently John got tired of the stalls and wandered away by himself, leaving Susan sandwiched between two fat old ladies, who each wanted the same flannel petticoat. She was so interested in their quarrel and in all the other wranglings that she didn't even hear Emily Goodenough's cries of 'Time to go home, Miss Susan!'

But after a while she began to feel rather flattened by all the old ladies, and she wandered off in the direction of the shrubbery.

Now, the vicarage garden was one of those particularly nice ones that are full of little unexpected dents and hollows and square green lawns—each one kept a secret from the other by thick, dark hedges. Susan was just going to push through the laurels that bordered a big circular lawn, when John came towards her.

He was looking as excited as though he had just found a bird's nest.

'Gummidge is here!' whispered John. 'Come and see, but don't make a sound, whatever you do!'

He dropped down on to his hands and knees, and began to crawl through the bushes. Susan followed him until only a thick branch of laurel hid her view of the lawn. John put his finger to his lips, and very, very softly pulled the branch back until Susan could see the wide stretch of grass.

Gummidge was there, sitting on a garden-roller. His legs were straddled, and he was making a queer, crooning sound. All round him, covering the grass so thickly that there was hardly a daisy to be seen, were rabbits. There were hundreds of them!

'Listen!' whispered John, and Susan kept so still that she could hear the strange, tearing noise of the rabbits all busy nibbling.

Sometimes one of them stopped, and pricked its pinkish ears, and sometimes one tried to hop over the backs of some of the others.

It was the most extraordinary sight that Susan had ever seen.

Every now and then, Gummidge changed the tune of his crooning. When he did this, the rabbits gathered themselves together and lolloped forward. The places they left were bitten close and clean.

'Ooh!' said Susan, forgetting to speak in a whisper. At the sound of her voice, one of the smallest rabbits sat up and looked about him. A dozen or so more followed his example; there they sat with their transparent pink ears blown back from their wild faces, while their noses twitched and nuzzled the air.

Gummidge crooned again, and they all began to nibble. The scarecrow stooped down, picked up a middle-aged rabbit, stroked its white stomach, gave its scut a friendly tweak, and plumped it down on the grass again.

'They've very nearly finished now,' whispered John.

'I *must* go and play with them,' said Susan, and she scrambled to her feet and ran out into the middle of the lawn. She was never quite certain afterwards about what really happened. She may have fallen over a rabbit. In a moment she was lying flat on the grass with John beside her, while baby, and old, and middle-aged rabbits scuttered across her back and over her shoulders. She felt their soft bodies tickling her neck, and she heard the frantic drumming of their feet.

When she stood up again every rabbit was gone, and Gummidge was sitting on the garden roller and whistling a dreary little tune to himself. The grass was as close and smooth as a tablecloth; there was not a blade out of place—not a daisy or buttercup anywhere.

The children felt suddenly shy of Gummidge. Up till then they had thought of him as a queer, silly thing, half scarecrow, half human. But his behaviour with the rabbits showed that he was a kind of wizard as well. They felt afraid.

'Morning!' shouted Gummidge, and when he showed his untidy teeth, they didn't feel shy any longer.

'How did you manage to cut the grass with rabbits?' asked John.

'I didn't,' replied Gummidge. 'I ate it with rabbits. Now, if I was a gardener, I'd be something like a gardener. I'd cut the hedges with cows, so I would, and I'd kill the worms with moles. There's no need for tools; they're clumsy things.'

'But gardeners don't like moles,' objected John.

'That's only because they aren't handy with them,' said Gummidge. 'Now, even rabbits takes a bit of managing, and as for a mole—' Here he stopped speaking, got up from the roller and began to move sideways across the lawn.

'Where are you going?' asked Susan.

'Goin' for my wages of course,' replied Gummidge. 'The vicar promised me half a crown to cut his lawn for him. He likes it done early, but he didn't know how I was going to do it.'

'Why don't you walk straight?' asked John crossly. The scarecrow's straw boots kept jabbing against his legs and they tickled horribly.

'If it comes to that, why don't you walk *sideways*?' retorted Gummidge.

'Why should we?' asked Susan.

'Slower!' said Gummidge. 'Makes a longer spring of it!' And as there really seemed to be no reply, the three continued to walk across the lawn.

Presently Susan sighed. 'I am so tired of the back of your head!' she said.

'And I'm tired and sick of your prickly boots,' said John. 'And I hate walking with someone who is looking into my ear all the time. I do wish you'd walk straight.'

He seized hold of one of Gummidge's arms as he spoke, and Susan took the other one. Between them they managed to get the scarecrow into a very nearly straightforward walking position.

'Talkin' of spring,' began Gummidge conversationally. 'Have you ever heard tell —' Then, before the children had time to be astonished at his extraordinary behaviour he had jerked his hands free from theirs, and lay in a dead sulk at their feet.

Susan, who had been walking with her head in the air, stumbled over the scarecrow's arm and fell flat on her face. So she didn't notice that Farmer Braithwaite, who had walked through one of the openings in the hedge, was staring at them angrily.

'Hey! How many times am I to tell you to leave that scarecrow alone?' he asked. 'Anyone would think you were daft to go dragging that thing over to the vicarage.'

'We didn't,' said Susan as she got up from the grass.

'Didn't you take it off the rubbish heap?'

'Well, sort of!' agreed Susan. 'But we didn't bring him here.'

'I suppose you'll tell me he walked,' went on Farmer Braithewaite in a particularly horrid way.

'If we say he did, then you'll say he didn't,' said John, who had decided that he simply would not be bullied. The farmer strode towards them, and prodded Gummidge with a stick.

'Oh, please don't do that!' begged Susan. 'He's had such a lot of trouble with his inside, already.'

'What's that, eh?' asked the farmer.

'The sparrows stole it,' explained John.

'Hey? The sparrows stole it?' repeated Farmer Braithewaite. 'The sparrows stole it, indeed! That is likely, that is! They flew with him and dropped him on to the lawn here, I suppose.'

'Oh dear!' said Susan despairingly. 'Why don't you even begin to try to understand? The sparrows hadn't anything to do with this afternoon. They only just—'

She was interrupted by a little cry from John.

'He's moving,' he said squeakily. 'He's coming out of his sulk. Look!'

Certainly Gummidge was stirring. Little rustly noises seemed to be coming from inside him. Susan distinctly saw his coat heave, as though he were breathing gently.

Yet his face was very turnipy and his legs and arms looked as stiff as hedge-stakes.

'Now perhaps you *will* believe us,' shouted Susan defiantly.

Farmer Braithewaite backed a few steps, then came nearer and bent over the scarecrow. The rustly noises continued, and the coat moved again.

'It's queer!' muttered the farmer. 'Ah! I thought so!' He whisked the corner of Gummidge's coat aside with his stick, and the children saw the ground stir in the place that had been covered.

'Mole!' said Farmer Braithewaite, and so it was. The little hillock of earth heaved for an instant, and two or three tiny streams of dust trickled down into the newly-made cracks. That was all. The stirring of Gummidge had only been caused by some small and probably obstinate mole, who had refused to be disturbed in the middle of his tunnelling.

Farmer Braithewaite made a sound that was

partly anger and partly grunt; then he stooped down and swung Gummidge on to his shoulder.

The scarecrow's head dangled limply down the farmer's back, flopping rakishly with each step. His ragged coat flapped rather sadly and little gusts of chaff blew out from his sleeves and swirled about in the breeze.

'It's lucky he's being carried pocket-up,' said Susan. 'Or I don't know what would happen to the nest.'

Chapter 7

'And now he really will be burned!' said Susan sadly. Then, remembering what Emily so often said, she added, 'I'm sure it's a warning to anybody not to sulk.'

But Gummidge was not burned, although he might have been if every stall had not been stripped bare, and if all the old ladies who had bought petticoats were not wishing that they had bought aprons instead. The truth was that all the guests at the vicarage were longing for even more exciting bargains. So when Farmer Braithewaite appeared on the lawn with Gummidge on his back, a shout went up from a group of lads: 'How much, Mister!'

'Let's sell the old scarecrow!' shouted Mrs Briggs. 'He'd scare the damp from my washing right enough.'

'Let's sell the scarecrow!' clamoured all the little children, and one of them added: 'We'll send him to school instead of Tony Higginsthwaite. Teacher would never notice the difference.'

Farmer Braithewaite hesitated, then he smiled. 'Let's sell the scarecrow!' he echoed, and he gave Gummidge a jerk that nearly sent his head spinning. Then before Susan or John could do or say anything, one of the men set Gummidge in a chair on the top of a trestle table. The postman seized a hammer and the auction began.

Gummidge was still looking most extraordinarily sulky and yet the rocking of the chair gave him a very life-like look, even though it did jolt his head in a rather terrifying manner.

Now nobody particularly wanted Gummidge, but everyone loves an auction sale, and so a great many people began to call out 'Sixpence!' 'A shilling!' 'One and sixpence!' in a very excited way. Some of them only nodded, though, and one old lady who was sitting alone on the front bench kept jerking her head violently.

Suddenly the chair, which had long since finished rocking, began again rather violently.

'He's coming alive!' whispered Susan to John. 'Do watch.'

John looked and he noticed that Gummidge's head was wagging slowly, as though he were trying to keep time with the swaying of the chair. Then, as he looked at him, Gummidge winked slowly and began to flap it in a feeble sort of way.

'Keep that chair still!' shouted Mrs Briggs. 'Keep that chair still. We want to look at what we're buying, don't we?'

'I never touched it,' replied the auctioneer angrily.

'Oh dear,' whispered Susan. 'I do hope Gummidge won't come alive while all these people are looking at him. It would be so awkward for him.'

'Can't *we* buy him?' asked John.

The children sat down on the grass and began to coax pennies out of their pig money boxes with a rusty knife blade.

But they were interrupted by a shout of 'Gone to Mrs Kibbins for five shillings!'

The old lady in the front bench sat up with a jerk.

'Eh?' she said.

'You've got the scarecrow,' shouted the postman.

'What's he say?' asked Mrs Kibbins. 'Does he say that I'm a scarecrow?'

'You've bought the scarecrow,' said the postman, and he carried the limp figure of Gummidge over to Mrs Kibbins.

'I've done no such thing,' she said.

'You've been nodding all the time,' said the postman. 'And a nod means a bid, as everyone knows!'

'Maybe you was asleep, Missus!' shouted little Tommy Higginsthwaite.

Now, as a matter of fact, Mrs Kibbins had been asleep during the sale, but she hated Tommy Higginsthwaite, who always stole her fruit, so she took five shillings out of her pocket, and said, 'I'll be very glad of that scarecrow; he'll help to keep two-legged birds out of my garden.'

'All birds is two-legged,' jeered Tommy Higginsthwaite. However, Mrs Kibbins simply turned her back on him, and seized hold of Gummidge by one of his broomstick arms. His legs trailed along the grass and his head flopped wearily on to his own rustling shoulder. And all the while Father Robin flew from bush to bush, crying 'Wife! Wife! Wife!' in such a distressed way that Susan rushed up to Mrs Kibbins and said, 'There's a robin's nest in his coat pocket. Do please be careful of it, and don't let Tommy Higginsthwaite see it.'

'Well now, did you ever,' exclaimed Mrs Kibbins, but as she was quite a kind old lady, she promised that she would be careful, and she turned Gummidge sideways so that the nest should not be crushed.

Father Robin paused in the middle of his circling, and perched for a second on Susan's shoulder as though to say 'Thank you!'

'I don't understand how the robins put up with Gummidge!' said John as the children walked back to the farm. 'Robins are generally so shy that if anyone touches their eggs they desert.'

'I expect Gummidge has explained to them,' replied Susan. 'He is rather magic, you know. I don't suppose that robins would mind if the trees they build in were to walk about. Gummidge is as much like a tree as he's like a person.'

'He's more like a turnip than anything,' said John. 'I wonder when he will come out of his sulk.'

It was quite a long time before the children were able to talk to Gummidge again. Every time they passed Mrs Kibbins's cottage, they peered over the wall. But though they whistled and coughed and even whispered 'Gummidge!' when nobody was about, he never answered them. He stood in the middle of Mrs Kibbins's potato patch. Every time the wind blew, he waved his raggedy arms dutifully, but his face was set and sulky and he never stirred his stiff lips, or opened the slits of his eyes, or showed the slightest sign of being anything but a very ordinary scarecrow.

'He must be furious at having been sold as if he was a common bag of coals,' said Susan. 'But after all it wasn't *our* fault. Do look at the way he's swinging round; he seems in the most frightful temper.'

Certainly Gummidge was more active than he had been in the days when he had stirred the rooks out of Ten-acre field, but that was because Mrs Kibbins had tied him to a broomstick which she planted in a sunken drainpipe. His straw boots were several inches above ground, and whenever the wind blew, he twisted round on his stick, so that sometimes he faced the village street and sometimes turned away from it. His back was nearly always turned when the children came to look at him. They wondered if he swung round on purpose, or if he was ordered entirely by the wind.

They longed to go into the garden and shake him out of his sulks, but it is difficult to go into gardens unless you know the owners of them rather well.

One day, when Susan had been taken into Penfold by Mrs Braithewaite, John wandered down the village street, and when he reached Mrs Kibbins's house he met the old lady coming out of her garden gate.

'I suppose,' said John, who had suddenly had an idea. 'I suppose you haven't any weeds in your garden?'

'There's always weeds in gardens,' retorted Mrs Kibbins. 'There's always weeds *and* children, and I don't know which is worst! They're both rampageous.'

'Oh!' said John, and then as there didn't seem to be any other reply, he muttered 'Oh!' again, and shuffled his feet. 'I suppose,' he said. 'I suppose you wouldn't like me to do any weeding for you?'

Mrs Kibbins looked at him suspiciously, but then you must remember that her garden had suffered terribly from Tommy Higginsthwaite, who lived next door. To her, one boy was as bad as another.

'Do you know weeds from flowers?' she asked.

'Well, I know groundsel and I know chickweed, and I know dandelions, when Susan isn't about; *she* thinks they are very specially nice flowers,' he answered. 'I'd like to weed your garden.'

'It don't seem natural,' murmured Mrs Kibbins. 'No, it don't seem natural for a boy to want to weed.'

'I don't generally,' explained John. 'But today I thought it might be rather fun to weed your garden.'

'Well, there's no harm in it that I can see,' said Mrs Kibbins. 'Tommy Higginsthwaite's trampled on the beds already and there's no fruit at this time of year. You can do a bit of weeding, if you like, while I go to Penfold.'

John dawdled along the garden path for as long as Mrs Kibbins was in sight, but as soon as her bonnet feathers had whisked round the corner, he crossed the little grass plot with its border of oyster shells and tiptoed across the potato patch, where Gummidge swung desolately in the wind.

'Good morning,' he said.

There was no reply, but perhaps this was not to be wondered at, since the scarecrow had his back to John, and his stick was creaking noisily in its drainpipe.

John walked round until he faced Gummidge, then he said 'Good morning!' again. This time there was a faint grunt in answer, and Gummidge raised an arm and drew his coat sleeve across his muddy face.

' 'Tisn't,' he said. 'It isn't a good morning except for worms and such-like. It's all dank and mizzling and giddy.'

'There isn't such a thing as a *giddy* morning!' objected John. 'You can't have a giddy morning.'

'Can't I?' repeated Gummidge miserably. 'Can't I? That's all you know about it. I've been giddy for a week now, twisting and turning and spinning, till I don't know which side of myself I'm on.'

Here the wind caught his arms, which were spread out like the sails of a windmill, and swung him round. When his indignant face appeared again, he continued, 'I'm as dizzy as a weathercock. It's not right.' The last words sounded faintly, because Gummidge's back was turned once more. 'It'll addle the eggs!' he went on, as he revolved again. 'It'll addle the eggs and then the young birds *will* look silly, won't they?'

'But there won't be any young birds if the eggs are addled,' said John, who guessed that Gummidge was talking of the robin's eggs. 'Addled eggs don't hatch out.'

'Some on 'em do,' said Gummidge. The wind had died down, and so he was able to keep still. 'Some on 'em do, and then the birds are daft. Cuckoos are all daft; it's in the family. But there, you can't expect eggs to keep steady when they're laid all over the place. Woodpeckers are daft too; they laugh at themselves all summer. Most tomtits are daft too; upside down or sideways it's all the same to them. I could tell you tales about addled—addled—addled, addled, addled— ADDLED EGGS!' He was caught in a perfect tempest of wind, and his words came out in jerks as his coat tails flaunted in the breeze. John began to feel quite dizzy himself. Then he thought of a plan to save Gummidge from giddiness. Scooping up several handfuls of earth, he pushed them into the drainpipe that held Gummidge's broomstick, and rammed them down until all was steady.

'That's better,' panted Gummidge gratefully. 'I don't know what I should have done with five daft robins in my pocket. Robins is trouble enough at the best of times, but when they're muddled from the start—' He broke off abruptly and asked, 'How's the field?'

'What field?'

'Ten-acre, of course.'

'I think it's all right,' replied John.

'Misses me, I guess,' said Gummidge. 'But if I stay here a bit, I'll learn quite a lot. Mrs Kibbins's daughter-in-law has a baby that takes my fancy. I like listening to the folks talking through the window in the evening. It's company for me. I'd like to hear a bit about the world afore I'm married.'

'Are you going to be married?' asked John in surprise. Somehow it was difficult to think of Gummidge as a husband.

'I'll be married some time,' replied Gummidge. 'The trouble is there's so few she-scarecrows hereabouts. Now there used to be one in the field next to Ten-acre, before it was set down for grazing. She wore a brown skirt and a Salvation Army bonnet and she had a set of real artificial teeth that had been sent to a rummage sale by the squire's housekeeper. I always hoped to share them, but she wouldn't look at me. Noo nye! She wouldn't look at me.'

'Why not?' asked John.

'Because her back was turned to me, of course,' said Gummidge. 'She was set in the field with her back to me.'

'Then what could you expect?' asked John.

'I didn't. I only wondered what her face was like. I used to cough to her in the evenings, and sometimes she'd champ her teeth at me. I heard them gnashing as plain as anything, when the wind was in the right mood.'

Gummidge sighed gustily and wiped his face with his coat sleeve.

'It was beautiful to hear her teeth,' he

continued. 'Ooh aye, it was beautiful while it lasted. You'd never guess how lonesome I were when they took her away on a cart.'

'Where did they take her to?' asked John.

'How should I know?' asked Gummidge gloomily. 'Maybe they took her to London. She was a mighty good scarer too. You'd understand what I felt like if you'd ever heard her rattling her imitation teeth. I'm fond of love, I am. I'll tell you a secret. Some day I'm going to look for that she-scarecrow; some day, when I know who I belongs to.'

'But don't you know?'

'How should I? Bits of me belonged to different folks to begin with; then I was sold to Mrs Kibbins. Who do I belong to? That's what I want to know.'

'You belong to yourself, of course.'

'Then I ought to have that five shillings that was paid for me,' said Gummidge reasonably. 'Where is it?'

But John couldn't answer that question, and just as Gummidge's face was beginning to settle itself into a sulky expression there was a click of the gate. John, remembering that he was supposed to be weeding, began to grub up a particularly tough dandelion. However, the creaking of perambulator wheels told him that the gate had been opened by young Mrs Kibbins, who had been taking her baby for an airing. She went into the house without taking any notice of John. Presently Gummidge wheezed, 'Have you got a knife?'

'Yes,' replied John. 'And it's got a corkscrew in it.'

'I don't want that,' said Gummidge. 'That's a dizzy sort of thing. I want to cut these pesky ropes.' He fidgeted with the strands of tarred string that bound him to the post.

'I'll cut them,' said John.

'I'll cut them myself, when the time comes. Maybe I'll want to go for a walk, but it wouldn't do for Mrs Kibbins to see me loose.'

'I'd better cut the string round your feet,' said John. 'You can't reach it while your middle is tied to the broomstick, and if you do it afterwards you'll fall on your face.'

' 'Twouldn't do it no harm!' muttered Gummidge. But at last he allowed John to cut the string round his ankles. Then he pocketed the knife, and, raising his legs in the air, until he looked as though he was sitting in an invisible chair, he closed his eyes.

Once again the garden gate creaked, and John jumped up from the ground. He looked at Gummidge's legs. Surely Mrs Kibbins would notice something queer about them if she happened to peep out of her window. He rushed to the scarecrow and tried to pull his legs downwards. They were terribly stiff and felt quite jointless. He pulled again. This time they creaked horribly, but luckily the closing of the garden gate covered the sound. John tugged and tugged until he was nearly breathless. All the time he heard the sound of Mrs Kibbins's boots click-clacketing up the flagged path. Once more he pulled, and this time Gummidge's legs straightened suddenly downwards, with a jerk that sent John on to his back. He had only just time to pull up a piece of groundsel before Mrs Kibbins walked across the potato patch.

'Have you pulled up many weeds?' she said pleasantly.

'I've pulled up this one,' said John. He hoped that Mrs Kibbins wouldn't notice how hot and breathless and untidy he was.

Mrs Kibbins looked at the groundsel. 'Is that all?' she asked.

'Well, it's a very nice one, isn't it?' stammered John. 'It's got a nice big root. It's better than nothing. Emily says that every little helps.'

He felt that he must keep on talking in case

Mrs Kibbins should notice that Gummidge's feet were untied.

Mrs Kibbins looked scornfully at the weed. 'It's little enough,' she said sourly.

John was glad to say goodbye and go home.

Chapter 8

After the affair of the single groundsel root, John did not dare to ask Mrs Kibbins if he might weed her garden again, and since there was no possible excuse for going into it, the children could only peep at Gummidge as they went down the village street. His back was always turned to them, for nobody had removed the earth that John had stuffed into the drainpipe.

'If you'd had any sense,' grumbled Susan, 'if you had had any sense at all, you would have turned Gummidge's face to the street. I do want to see if he's still sulking.'

It certainly was dreadfully tantalizing not to be able to see Gummidge's nice, knobbly face.

'You'd never think that we were once friends, would you?' said Susan sadly as they walked down the village. 'You'd never think——' But she suddenly stopped grumbling, and cried, 'Oh! Gypsies! Look!'

A painted yellow van was rumbling and rattling down the street. Running by the side of it was a lurcher dog, and sitting on the flap at the back was a row of gypsy children. Their eyes were as black and bright as elderberries, and they had mischievous, monkey faces. A blue van followed the yellow one. Then came a scarlet van with a golden roof. Each was pulled by a skewbald pony with jingling harness. Queer smells of stew and rabbit skins and oily leather filtered out through the open doorways of the vans.

'I'm glad we've finished with whooping-cough,' said Susan. That morning Emily had told them that they were not infectious any longer.

'It must be splendid to be a gypsy,' said John.

'Yes,' agreed Susan. 'It must be lovely to wear golden rings in your ears and to have hens laying eggs for you all over the place, and to be able to go anywhere and never come back at all.'

The whole village seemed to be excited about the gypsies. Heads bobbed in and out of the upstairs windows of the cottages. Children ran out of doors and munched hunks of bread and jam, as the gypsies went by. Even the washing on the clothes lines seemed excited. Pyjama legs and pink flannelette nightdresses puffed themselves out, and tugged at the clothes lines, as though they too longed to follow the gypsies.

After that Susan and John forgot all about Worzel Gummidge for several hours. They followed the caravans to the edge of the common, and listened to the hammering in of tent-pegs and the clattering of iron stewpans, until it was time for dinner.

Emily Goodenough told them that the annual fair always came very early to Scatterbrook.

'The place'll be half daft,' she grumbled. 'What with all the merry-go-rounds and swing-boats and such-like rubbish, there'll be no work done for a week. And, as if that wasn't enough, Mrs Bloomsbury-Barton is arranging a village baby show. There's to be a whist drive at the vicarage too. It all means that there won't be a lass to help with the spring cleaning. I don't know what the world's coming to.'

'I wish we could take Gummidge to the fair,' said Susan as soon as Emily Goodenough had turned her back. 'I'm sure a ride on a merry-go-round would be a treat for him.'

'It would only make him giddy,' said John wisely. 'And then he'd probably sulk, and we should have to pay for all his turns until he had stopped being cross.'

'Well, I think we ought to tell him about the fair,' persisted Susan. 'Let's go and look at him.'

When they reached Mrs Kibbins's garden wall and peeped over it, they saw at once that something had happened to Gummidge. His coat-sleeves were flapping more limply than usual, and, instead of standing straight out from his shoulders, they hung down. His trousers sagged dismally.

'What has happened to him?' asked John.

'I don't know,' replied Susan. 'But he looks quite different, doesn't he?'

Suddenly she gave a little cry and clutched John's arm.

'Isn't his hat twiddling about very queerly? And look, there's a gap between it and his coat collar. He hasn't got a neck at all! Somebody's taken his head away. How very, very, *very* horrid of them!'

She burst into tears.

'Nobody would take his head away,' said

John. 'Nobody would want it; it isn't pretty enough.'

All the same he felt rather frightened himself, as he looked at the length of polished broomstick that bridged the space between Gummidge's hat and collar.

'I can't bear it!' sobbed Susan. 'If he's been executed, it means that he is dead.'

'Scarecrows are never executed.'

'You never know what might happen to a person like Gummidge,' wailed Susan. 'And I'd got so fond of him. I even loved his knobbles and his toothy grin and the bit of mud where his ear ought to have been. I'd got used to his sulks and everything. He's the first grown-up friend we've ever had who didn't order us about.'

If Mrs Kibbins hadn't chanced to come out of her door at that moment, the children would certainly have gone into the garden to look more closely at Gummidge. But Mrs Kibbins's bonnet feathers were waving rather fiercely, and her nose looked so hooky, that Susan, who could not see very clearly through her tears, sobbed: 'I think she's a witch! I think she's done something very, very beastly to my darling Gummidge!' Then, before John could stop her, she turned and ran like a rabbit up the village street. She only stopped for breath when she reached the corner of

Ten-acre field. Then she flung herself down on to the grass and sobbed miserably.

John felt rather choky himself. He tried to think that everything was all right, and that the disappearance of the head was only one of Gummidge's queer ways.

'After all,' he said. 'After all, Gummidge may have pocketed his head!'

'Why should he?' asked Susan.

'To keep it warm, perhaps.'

'How silly you are,' said Susan. Then she shivered, and whimpered, 'I'm most dreadfully cold.'

'Let's go home,' suggested John.

'I don't want to go home. And I don't want to see anyone,' wailed Susan. 'If we hadn't known Gummidge so well, we might have enjoyed having a funeral with him. But now everything is perfectly beastly.'

'Perhaps somebody is making a new face for Gummidge,' said John.

'He wouldn't be the same with a new face. He couldn't be the same without that knobbly nose.'

Susan stood up and rubbed her wet face with her muddy hand. Then she trailed dismally along the little lane that led to the foot of the hills.

'I'd like to make him a wreath,' she said. 'Do worzels have flowers? I'm sure he would like a wreath of worzel blossom better than anything else.'

'You don't think a cow could have eaten his head, do you?' asked John. 'Cows do eat turnips, you know, and Gummidge's face was very turnipy.'

'There aren't any cows in Mrs Kibbins's garden,' replied Susan. 'I'm so afraid that she has *boiled* his head.'

They were passing the little empty, single-roomed cottage that stood at the foot of the Beacon Hill as Susan spoke, and she stopped to gather a sprig of the woodruff that grew by the tumbledown gate.

Suddenly she heard a cough—a queer, husky cough that could only belong to a sheep or to Gummidge.

'He's there!' she cried. 'Perhaps he's put himself together again.'

'He couldn't have done that,' objected John. 'It can't really be Gummidge; perhaps it's a tramp.'

'Listen!' said Susan again, and she held up her finger. From inside the cottage there came the most peculiar crooning sound and presently they were able to make out the words—

'Hushaby Scarey,
Don't be contrary!

Turnips will nip you unless you are good!
Worzels will worzel,
And furzles will furzle;
Bogles will fetch you, unless you are good.'

'Gummidge!' shouted John. 'That's Gummidge's voice!' He burst open the door and rushed inside.

There was no furniture in the cottage, but only a wooden packing-case. Gummidge was sitting on this. In his arms was a small baby, as raggedy and disreputable looking as himself. Gummidge was dressed even more peculiarly than usual. Instead of a coat, he wore starched blue overalls that had gone limp in patches, brown cotton stockings, and real boots, but his face was unchanged and his grin was as wide as ever.

'Hush!' said Gummidge, and he held up a reproving finger. 'Don't wake the baby.'

'We thought you were dead,' cried Susan.

'Not I!' said Gummidge. 'I don't do things like that in a hurry. I'm a slow mover, I am.'

'But we saw you in Mrs Kibbins's garden about half an hour ago,' said John. 'Your head was gone.'

'Of course it were,' said Gummidge. 'It were on me, and I've been here all the morning. I don't go leaving my head about. I were brought up to be tidy, I were.'

'Were you really?' asked John. Susan felt angry with him; she wanted to find out all about the baby, but she daren't interrupt for fear Gummidge would sulk.

'Well, in some ways I were brought up to be tidy,' said Gummidge modestly. 'I mayn't be *extra* tidy. My old nurse said to me, years an' years ago, she said, "Don't you go leaving your head and arms and legs about. It causes trouble and makes it difficult to sort yourself afterwards."'

'Why are you dressed like that?' asked John, though Susan kicked him hard.

'Just to make a nice change!' said Gummidge airily. 'And to give the robin a rest. Mrs Kibbins left the overall in the wash-house. It fits me a treat.'

'That was stealing,' said Susan primly.

'I left the straw boots behind instead,' said Gummidge. 'And I got these boots and trousers from a friend.' He stuck out his legs and looked at his boots proudly. 'Leastways he might have been a friend, if we'd ever got to know him. But it seemed a shame to wake him up, when he was sleeping so soundly. We can see about being friends later!'

The baby stirred and opened its rather muddled-looking eyes. Its face, like Gummidge's, was remarkably turnipy-looking, for all its features seemed to have melted into one another. Susan noticed with relief that it did not wear bottle straws on its grubby little feet.

'Whose is it?' she asked.

'Well,' said Gummidge, slowly. 'I *call* it mine.'

'But *is* it yours?' asked Susan. Really, she would not have been surprised to hear anything.

'Now you're asking,' said Gummidge. 'I don't know, and you don't know, and it doesn't know. I found it in the wood.'

'Was it *growing* there?' asked Susan curiously. She felt that Gummidge's baby had probably sprung up in the night like a mushroom, so singularly root-like was its face. It puckered it now in the most dreadfully ugly manner. Gummidge snatched a wisp of straw from his neck and began to tickle its face until it giggled. He certainly had a way with babies.

'Was it growing!' persisted Susan.

'Now, how should I know?' asked Gummidge pettishly. 'They grow so slow, you can't seem to catch them at it. And *how* they grow beats me! I can understand a snake; *that* casts its skin when it grows out of it. But your sort might be made of elastic, the way they stretches out into men and women. You'll do it yourselves!'

'Is it a baby *scarecrow*?' asked John.

'It'll scare the crows all right when it yells,'

said Gummidge, and he held the baby up. 'Like to hear it?' he asked.

'No!' shouted John. 'What are you going to do with it?'

'Eddicate it,' replied Gummidge firmly. 'Eddicate it, until it's a nice companion for me.'

'But you can't keep a baby out in the fields all night,' said Susan.

'Can't I?' said Gummidge defiantly. 'Can't I? That's all you know about it.'

'It'll die,' said John.

'Shan't let it,' said Gummidge. 'This baby's got to learn to do as it's told, same as the rabbits do.' He rocked it violently backwards and forwards in his arms as he spoke. 'Anyway,' he added. 'Anyway, I've finished with rook-scaring for the present. I'm going to take a bit of holiday. Ooh aye. Now give over, Scarey,' he said, as the baby began to pucker its face again.

'Let me nurse it,' begged Susan, and she sat down on the floor and spread out her skirts to make a lap.

Rather reluctantly, Gummidge laid the baby in her arms. It had a very queer face and the tufts of hair that stuck up from its head were rather like Gummidge's own green sprouts.

'Is it a boy?' asked John.

'I dare say,' replied Gummidge indifferently.

'How old is it?' asked Susan.

'Maybe eight months, but it's difficult to tell unless you've been with them all along.'

'You can't keep it out all night in Mrs Kibbins's garden,' said Susan anxiously.

'I wasn't going to,' replied Gummidge. 'Young Mrs Kibbins's daughter might take a fancy to it and change it over for her own. I like the colour of this one best, though hers is all right. There's cows hereabouts. I can get a drop of milk for it when it wants it, and there's straw here to make it a bed.' He looked round the cottage with a beaming smile.

'It's rather a rough sort of place,' said Susan.

'This baby's got to be brought up rough,' said Gummidge.

All the same, the children noticed that he handled the baby quite gently as he took it from Susan's lap.

'Let me have it,' said Susan. 'I'm sure I know much more about babies than you do.'

A slow, sulky expression came over Gummidge's face. He put the baby behind his back and looked at her defiantly.

Susan guessed from its yells that it was being held upside-down, and she sprang to her feet rather angrily.

'Now see here,' said Gummidge. 'See here; if you want a baby, you must go and find one for yourself. There's lots about.'

'But you'll hurt it,' objected John.

'It's more likely to hurt itself, the way it's going on,' replied Gummidge. But all the same he whisked the baby round again on to his lap, and began to tickle its face.

'*Do* let me,' pleaded Susan.

'Now see here,' said Gummidge. 'See here. You'll make me desert if you go on like that. A lot of birds would have given up long ago.'

'But you aren't a bird,' argued John.

'In a manner of speaking, I am,' retorted Gummidge. 'I'm a special sort of crow—a *scare*-crow, just as a hedge-sparrow is a special sort of sparrow. One scares and t'other one hedges. Where's the difference?'

'I'm quite sure there *is* a difference,' said Susan, who was feeling most dreadfully muddled.

Gummidge's face went pale green with temper.

'You've drove me to it,' he said. 'I *will* desert!' And, still clutching the baby, he rose to his feet.

'Oh, *please* don't,' said Susan. 'We'll go away and leave you.'

Gummidge sat down jerkily.

'Goodbye,' he said. 'You can come and see me again when the baby's fledged.'

'Fledged!' repeated John.

'Haired, then,' said Gummidge. 'Haired and unwrinkled, since you're so particular.'

Then, because he looked very angry again, the children ran out of the cottage and home to tea.

Chapter 9

The annual Fair was a feast day in Scatterbrook, and on the morning before it began the village common looked like the green-carpeted nursery of some untidy baby giant who had left his playthings—tents, games, and toy people—littered about all higgledy-piggledy.

Early in the morning John and Susan had set out to pay a visit to Gummidge, but when they turned to look back on the village and saw all the excitement of preparation and heard the thrilling sound of tent-pegs being hammered into hard ground, and the ring and jingle of the merry-go-rounds, they decided to leave Gummidge to his sulks.

Mysterious things seemed to be happening on the common. Susan decided that the gypsies didn't look as excited as they ought to do. They were standing about in little groups and clusters. One of the women was talking to the policeman, who was scratching his head a great deal, as he always did when worried. One little girl was standing near, and she interrupted every now and then by whimpering, 'I couldn't help it, could I now?'

Susan knew exactly how she was feeling, as soon as she heard her speak, and, when she saw the child's very dirty face was streaked with the tracks of clean tears, she went up to her, and asked, 'What's the matter?'

However, the child only scuffled her feet on the grass, repeated, 'I couldn't help it, could I?' turned her back on Susan, and began to bite her nails.

Before there was time to ask any more questions, Emily came bustling across the common. She beckoned to the children, and as they could see at once that she was in a good temper, they rushed to meet her.

'There's a treat for you,' said Emily in her most mysterious voice.

'For me!' asked John.

'No, not for you.'

'For me! For me!' said Susan, dancing about as she always did when she was excited.

'You're going to the baby show this afternoon, and what do you think—?'

'Baby! Baby!' interrupted John. 'I always said Susan was a baby!'

Emily took no notice of him; she went on talking to Susan. 'There is going to be a baby show in the village hall, and Mrs Bloomsbury-Barton is going to be the judge, and give the prizes away.' Susan looked puzzled, and John was just going to interrupt again, when Emily gave him one of her don't-try-to-be-so-silly glances.

'Mrs Parsons has just been round to say that she would like you to present the bouquet to Mrs Bloomsbury-Barton.'

'What bouquet?' asked Susan.

'*The* bouquet.' Emily sounded very important. Secretly she was rather proud of John and Susan, though she didn't often let them know it, and she was very pleased because Susan had been chosen by Mrs Parsons to take part in the show.

'You'll have to have dinner early,' she continued. 'Because the baby show begins at half-past two, and I shall have to get you into your best dress. It's lucky you've lost your cough.'

Poor Susan felt dreadfully disappointed; she had hoped the treat would be a real treat and not something that meant wearing a best dress and party manners.

'But I don't like Mrs Bloomsbury-Barton,' she argued, 'and I don't want to give her anything.'

'I'm sure Mrs Bloomsbury-Barton is a very nice lady.' Emily sounded quite huffy. 'Now come along and don't be a rude, ungrateful little girl.'

'I don't see why *I* should be grateful when Mrs Bloomsbury-Barton's having the present!' argued Susan.

'And what am I going to do?' asked John.

'You're going too,' said Emily firmly.

It took quite a long time to get the children ready for the baby show, and they were so cross about it all that they weren't very helpful. Susan's arms were as stiff as Gummidge's when Emily made her try on the best dress, and John made a great fuss about washing the inside of his hands.

The tuck had to be let out of Susan's dress, and some chocolate stains had to be sponged off John's best coat.

When the baby show actually began, Susan rather enjoyed it. All the babies were so very pink and plump and clean and gurgly. Most of them enjoyed being put into the weighing baskets. But they didn't enjoy Mrs Bloomsbury-Barton at all.

When she looked at them, they puckered their faces into pleats, and yelled.

'Babies are cleverer than I thought,' muttered John.

Then, when the last baby had been weighed, the door of the hall opened, and in walked Mrs Kibbins. Behind her came her daughter pushing a perambulator.

Now, Mrs Kibbins was the proudest woman in the village. She thought that her little granddaughter was the finest baby in the county, just as she thought that her garden was the best in all Scatterbrook. She looked rather fiercely at all the other mothers and babies before she stooped over the perambulator and began to remove the blanket that covered the baby. Certainly the perambulator was the grandest in Scatterbrook; it had a white coverlet embroidered with blue forget-me-nots, and the blanket was as downy as young chickens. Mrs Kibbins shook it out proudly and folded it up very, very slowly.

'Let me help,' begged Mrs Bloomsbury-Barton, who was in a hurry for her tea.

'It's a baby show, not a blanket show,' whispered the mother of the thinnest baby. Mrs Kibbins's daughter did nothing at all. Her name was Mrs Turnpike, and she was frightened of her mother.

'Sakes!' said Mrs Kibbins, and she started back.

But Mrs Bloomsbury-Barton took no notice of her remark. She whisked the coverings aside and lifted out a small and rather odd-looking baby.

'A *dear* little creature!' murmured Mrs Bloomsbury-Barton, who made the same remarks about every child.

'Sakes!' repeated Mrs Kibbins.

But Mrs Bloomsbury-Barton, who was delighted to find a quiet baby, made a particularly foolish, crooning sound, and sat down on a chair with the baby on her lap.

All the other mothers crowded round her.

'Sakes!' said Mrs Kibbins. 'It's not yours, is it, Maud?' Mrs Turnpike shook her head drearily.

Nobody noticed except Susan and John, for everyone was staring in amazement at the baby. It was dressed most peculiarly. Nearly every garment was put on either upside down, back to front, or inside out, and each was in the wrong order.

When Mrs Bloomsbury-Barton began to dandle it, two chunks of turnip fell down on to her lap. She turned severely to Mrs Turnpike.

'I know that it is very difficult to find time for everything,' she said. 'Nobody knows better than I the trouble that a young baby can be.'

'It's not our Emmeline,' screamed Mrs Kibbins. 'I never set eyes on it before.'

'It's a changeling, that's what it is, Mrs Kibbins,' said the postmistress.

'Whose is it?' shouted Mrs Kibbins, and she looked angrily round the room.

'Diddums!' crooned Mrs Bloomsbury-Barton, for by this time the baby's face was almost knotted with rage, and it was kicking its muddy legs.

'Somebody's been playing a joke on me,' said Mrs Kibbins. 'And I've my own idea who it was, too!'

John looked at Susan, and Susan looked at John. The same terrible thought had come into their minds. The baby on Mrs Bloomsbury-Barton's lap was the baby that Gummidge had hidden in the empty cottage.

'I know!' quavered Mrs Turnpike. 'I know, it was you that did it, Mrs Higginsthwaite.'

'I never did,' said Mrs Higginsthwaite indignantly.

'Babies don't change *themselves*,' said Mrs Kibbins. 'I know when it was done too. We'd got baby ready and put her in the pram in the wash-house while we went up to tidy ourselves. Someone must have come and changed the babies then. I never looked under the coverlet because I thought Emmeline was asleep. I'm going to see who *has* got our Emmeline.' She walked across the room to the row of perambulators and began to search for Emmeline. Then she stared hard into the faces of all the babies in arms.

The policeman's wife stood up. 'I don't know if I ought to say,' she announced. 'I don't know if I ought to say, but my husband told me that one of the gypsies has lost a baby, too. That there looks like a tinker's brat to me. There's queer goings on in Scatterbrook.'

The baby gave a sudden yell, and began to wriggle violently. The sound of its crying woke up the washerwoman's twins, and they too began to scream. The noise became deafening. Mrs Kibbins ran round the room like a flustered bantam hen, and once more continued to search for Emmeline.

'Let me have the baby,' begged Susan, and, after one look at its furious face, Mrs Bloomsbury-Barton put it into her arms.

There was no doubt at all, so Susan decided; it was Gummidge's baby. She remembered a tiny red mark under its left eye, and there was no mistaking the peculiar tuftiness of its hair. The baby may possibly have remembered her, or it may have found her lap more comfortable than Mrs Bloomsbury-Barton's; anyway, it stopped crying and stared up at her in an unblinking manner.

'There's a bit of straw behind its ear,' remarked John.

'It's face is all muddied,' wailed Mrs Kibbins. Then she suddenly swooped down on the baby and picked it up from Susan's lap.

'It's wearing Emmeline's clothes,' she shouted. 'Oh dear! Oh dear! Oh dear!' Then she cried so noisily that every baby in the room began to wail again.

Suddenly the door opened and Tommy Higginsthwaite rushed into the room. As he was quite breathless, and as his mouth was full of toffee, it was some moments before he could speak. At last he gasped: 'You're wanted, Mrs Turnpike. My mother's found your Emmeline in the wash-house and she's dressed in a bit of sacking!'

'Sakes!' cried Mrs Kibbins, and, plumping the baby on to Mrs Bloomsbury-Barton's lap, she rushed out of the hall. Mrs Turnpike followed her.

The baby looked in disgust at Mrs Bloomsbury-Barton. Mrs Bloomsbury-Barton looked in disgust at the baby.

'Dear little thing!' she said at last. 'I wonder what we had better do with it?'

Nobody seemed to know, and one by one the mothers slipped away. The truth was that each was afraid of being left with the baby. When the last perambulator had creaked through the door, Mrs Bloomsbury-Barton rose to her feet.

Then Susan remembered the bouquet. There, on a wooden chair, lay something that looked like spinach and eggs. Unfortunately, the village postmistress, who was the fattest woman in Scatterbrook, had been sitting on the daffodils. Susan picked up the bunch of squashed flowers and handed it to Mrs Bloomsbury-Barton, and made a little curtsy.

Mrs Bloomsbury-Barton looked at the bunch as though it were a dead rabbit; she looked at the baby as though it were an even deader rabbit.

'How very, very kind,' she murmured. 'Will you carry them for me, dear? I suppose I must take this unfortunate mite home with me. It is all very sad.'

Two or three gypsies were loitering about the village street when Mrs Bloomsbury-Barton, Susan, and John walked out of the hall. Mrs Bloomsbury-Barton carried the baby awkwardly, for she felt ashamed of it and so tried to hide it under her cloak. The baby naturally disliked this. Possibly it was ashamed of Mrs Bloomsbury-Barton. It began to writhe and wriggle, to screw its face into knots, and to behave more like a caterpillar than a human child. Finally, it gave a terrific yell. The most raggedy of the gypsy women looked up at the sound of its voice, caught sight of the infuriated and dirty little face that was peeping through the fringe of Mrs Bloomsbury-Barton's cloak, and ran across the road.

She stood with her arms akimbo in front of Mrs Bloomsbury-Barton, who looked at her haughtily.

'Where did you get that baby from?' demanded the gypsy. Then she whisked the fringe from the child's face. 'It's mine!' she shouted, and snatched it fiercely from Mrs Bloomsbury-Barton's arms. The baby nestled its muddy face contentedly against its mother's shawl. The gypsy raised her voice and shouted, 'Here's the woman that stole my baby!' For the next few minutes Susan and John felt as though they were in the middle of a particularly fierce dog-fight. All the gypsies began to shout abuse at Mrs Bloomsbury-Barton, the baby yelled, and the villagers came out of their cottages and joined in the dispute. The trouble was that Mrs Bloomsbury-Barton was not allowed to explain. Every time she opened her mouth, one or other of the gypsies shouted her down.

'We'll have the law on you,' said one.

'Thieving hussy!' screeched another.

Susan and John began to feel quite sorry for Mrs Bloomsbury-Barton, who was finding it terribly difficult to be dignified. Presently the policeman joined the crowd, and then Mrs Kibbins, and Mrs Turnpike, who was now carrying the real Emmeline, came out of their cottage.

In the middle of all the confusion and excitement Emily Goodenough came running down the village street and called the children home to tea.

Afterwards, Susan heard that Mrs Bloomsbury-Barton had had great difficulty in pacifying the gypsies. She had not come out of her prim house again for quite a long time.

Chapter 10

The next day Susan and John went early to the common. They rode on the merry-go-rounds, rocked themselves giddy on the swing-boats, shied at coconuts, ate liquorice bootlaces, and forgot all about Gummidge and the baby. They paid pennies to see the fat lady, who wore a pink satin dress quite early in the morning, and who sat all day long in a stuffy little tent.

Mrs Braithewaite had given the children some sandwiches to eat out of doors. They had hidden these on the sunny side of a blackthorn hedge that bounded the common.

Ever since about half-past ten, John had kept on saying, 'It must be time for lunch. I do think we ought to picnic now, just in case we don't feel like it later on.'

'Why shouldn't we feel like it?' asked Susan.

'I've eaten such an awful lot of pink sugar mice,' explained John. 'And I think the mice would like some sandwiches; they can have a picnic inside *us* while we have a picnic out of doors.'

'What a very, very horrid idea,' said Susan.

But by eleven o'clock she began to feel hungry too, and so they left the hoop-la stall and set off for the blackthorn hedge.

They hunted for their lunch in and out of the hedgerow and all among the tufts of grass. They even thrust their arms deep down into rabbit burrows.

'A gypsy must have stolen it,' said John.

After that they very nearly quarrelled, for Susan said that she was quite sure that they had left the picnic basket behind a further hedge and insisted on going to look.

When they reached the other hedge they heard a sort of sucking noise, that was followed by some very loud gulps.

'I think someone is not eating very prettily,' remarked Susan as she scrambled through a gap in the hedge.

There, with his back to a hawthorn bush, sat Worzel Gummidge. He was holding the tail of a pink sugar mouse between two of his rather straggly teeth. Its body joggled against his chin, as he nibbled listlessly.

'Good morning,' said John.

'Umm!' mumbled Gummidge.

He jerked up his head, opened his mouth, and caught the mouse quite neatly.

'Good morning,' said Susan.

Gummidge pointed to his bulging cheek, shook his finger at her in a reproving manner, and began to crunch viciously. The children noticed that one of his boots was unfastened and that he was wearing the lace of it bound very tightly round the sleeve of his blue overall.

'Why do you wear your bootlace on your arm?' asked Susan.

Gummidge gave a final scrunch, and then a gigantic swallow, before replying sadly, 'I'm in mourning, I am.'

'Why?'

'I've lost my baby. Ooh aye. It does seem a pity, just as I'd got used to its crying.'

'It isn't dead, is it?' asked Susan in horror.

'Might as well be for all the use it is to me. Its mother's stolen it. And I only deserted it for a minute or two.'

'What happened?' asked Susan.

'Well, I'd taken it for a walk and I happened to be passing Mrs Kibbins's and I thought there might be a bit of blue in the wash-house, so I went in to look. Nobody noticed me and there was a perambulator inside, with a baby in it. Well, I thought Scarey would look a treat in a perambulator. And then I thought the other baby's clothes looked better than hers, so I took 'em off it and dressed Scarey in 'em. I'd just covered her up in the perambulator when I heard Mrs Kibbins coming.'

'Oh!' said Susan. 'Then it *was* you all the time?'

''Course it were,' agreed Gummidge. 'It wasn't me only some of the time. Well, when I heard Mrs Kibbins coming, I hid behind the mangle with the other baby, and waited until she'd wheeled the pram away. And that was the last I ever saw of Scarey.'

He sniffed sadly. 'It's a job being a scarecrow I can tell you.'

'I'm sure it must be,' agreed Susan. 'But why do you try to do so much?'

'Things just happens,' said Gummidge sadly. Then he added mournfully, 'It's all such a come-down.'

'What is!' asked John.

'Scaring sparrows instead of rooks.'

'Oughtn't you to be at work now?'

'There, now you've gone and spoiled it all,' shouted Gummidge angrily. 'There was I trying to think of happy things like pink sugar mice and you go on like that.'

'What's the matter!' asked John.

Gummidge's face slowly swelled into peevish bumps and knobbles. Then he took another pink sugar mouse out of a paper bag, and began to crumble it between his fingers.

'It makes me come over all queer to think of it,' he answered. 'I've come over as queer as merry-go-rounds—all dizzy like!' He hiccuped loudly.

'You shouldn't do that,' said Susan reprovingly. 'It's rude!'

'I *am* rude,' said Gummidge. Two pale-green tears trickled down his cheeks. 'I wants to be rude. It's not fair.'

'What isn't fair?' asked John.

'Being a nephew,' answered Gummidge. 'Now *she* enjoys being an aunt.'

'Who does?' enquired Susan patiently.

'Aunt, of course, my Aunt Sally. Oh! how I hates her. How I hates her. How I hates her,' Gummidge threw the bits of mouse at a sod of earth.

'Aunt Sally,' repeated Susan. 'Is she your aunt?'

The children had seen an Aunt Sally at the fair already. She was a very tall wooden lady, who stood on three legs before a canvas screen, while all the little boys of the village threw sticks at her. Susan remembered Aunt Sally's brightly painted face and her big bonnet and chintz dress, but she had never thought of her as a real *aunt*.

'Is *your* aunt a wooden one?' asked Gummidge. It was the first question he had ever really asked them. Susan was rather startled by it. So far Gummidge had seemed to take them for granted.

'Of course she isn't,' said John.

'Wooden ones is worst of all. They don't mind anything. You can kick 'em and pinch 'em and throw things at 'em, and they don't feel anything. The only thing you *can* do is to burn 'em. I wish I'd had a match this morning. But there! If I had had one she'd only have blown it out. She's so spiteful.'

'Well, you couldn't expect her to sit still while you set fire to her, could you?' asked Susan.

'The Guys do,' said Gummidge. 'I've never known a Guy as didn't.'

'But why do you hate her so?' persisted John. 'She doesn't look bad.'

'She's so spiteful and meddlesome,' replied Gummidge. 'I hates her. Ooh aye, I hates her as much as worms hates ducklings. If I could find a hatchet I'd chop her up. I daren't stay here any longer, or she'll come round and order me about again. She wants me to—' Here he broke off and began to sob loudly.

Susan patted his knobbly shoulder. 'What does she want you to do?' she asked.

'There you go reminding me of it again,' choked Gummidge. He got up, and the children saw that his face was all smeary because his tears had mixed with the dry dust on his face and had turned to moist mud.

'We'll look after you,' said John. 'We won't let anyone order you about.' He felt very grown-up indeed as he spoke. Then the three of them began to walk across the ploughland in the direction of the little spinney.

Gummidge's unlaced boot kept coming off, which rather delayed them. But he absolutely refused to untie the bootlace from his arm.

'I'm in mourning,' he persisted. 'I shall stay in mourning for ever and ever. I've a lot to mourn for, now that I've met Aunt again.'

'You don't mourn for people who are alive,' said Susan.

'We've cause to in our family,' snapped Gummidge.

'Where is she?' asked John, who rather wanted to talk to Aunt Sally.

'Where's she's not wanted, as like as not,' said Gummidge. 'I'm frightened of meeting her, but we should be safe in here.' He led the way through a gap in the hedge. As they rounded a holly bush he gave a sudden start that almost jerked his head off. He flung up one arm as he jumped, and now he stood with it sticking stiffly out from his shoulder, as though he were frozen.

'There's Aunt,' he quavered.

The children saw a curious sight. Sitting with her back to a tree was Gummidge's Aunt Sally. Two of her wooden legs rested on the ground, but the third stuck out stiffly above them. She wore an old-fashioned frock patterned with yellow daises, and a bonnet was perched on her painted, wooden hair. By her side was the children's picnic basket. She moved her arms, stiffly as a wooden doll, as she lifted the sandwich to her mouth. She had a hard, bright face, and her nose stuck out sharply.

'It's *her* right enough!' said Gummidge.

Aunt Sally took not the slightest notice of the children. She opened her mouth like a trap every time she bit, but in between each mouthful she pursed it up in the primmest manner.

'She does that so as not to get out of practice for holding the pipe,' whispered Gummidge.

'Don't whisper,' said Aunt Sally. Her voice was as creaky as a wooden rattle.

Gummidge and the children stood and stared at her.

'I think that's *our* dinner,' said Susan at last. She was feeling dreadfully hungry.

'Speak when you are spoken to,' rasped Aunt Sally.

'But it *is* our dinner,' said John, who was feeling even hungrier than Susan.

'Don't argue,' said Aunt Sally, and she took another bite. She seemed to enjoy the last sandwich very much. When she had finished she handed up the paper to Susan. 'Put it away tidily,' she said. Susan saw that she was wearing tight kid gloves. It was impossible not to obey Aunt Sally. Gummidge's friendly face was very melancholy. He began to move away.

'Don't fidget,' said Aunt Sally.

'Aunt,' muttered Gummidge. 'Aunt,' but he didn't seem able to say anything else.

'Why are you eating our dinner?' shouted John fiercely.

'Ask me no questions and I'll tell you no lies!' said Aunt Sally, and she snapped her teeth on a particularly large piece of cake.

'I do think she's horrid,' whispered Susan to John.

'Don't mutter!' said Aunt Sally. She spoke with such sudden fierceness that a large currant bounced out of her mouth. While she was hunting for this, John snatched an orange from the basket. Aunt Sally stretched out a long, thin arm and tweaked it away from him.

'If I had wished you to have any fruit I should have offered it to you,' she said. 'Worzel! you are poking your head.'

Gummidge jerked his head up so swiftly that for a minute or two it quivered like a ball on a post.

'Tell me the names of your friends,' continued Aunt Sally.

'I don't know,' muttered Gummidge. 'I never thought to ask. Names don't seem to matter to me. I knows folks by their faces.'

He looked so miserable that John said hastily, 'We are John and Susan.'

Aunt Sally looked at him disapprovingly, as though to say, 'I might have guessed it.' Then she began to peel the orange with her kid-gloved fingers.

'Why did you leave the Fair, Worzel?' asked Aunt Sally. 'It was extremely disobedient of you. In my young days nephews were taught to obey their elders.'

'You never had but one, and he was me,'

muttered Gummidge. He dropped his right arm to his side as he spoke, and stiffened sulkily.

'Don't sulk,' said Aunt Sally.

Worzel Gummidge pouted bulgily.

Suddenly Aunt Sally stood up with a curious tilting movement, and walked towards her nephew. Her front leg moved as though it worked by a hinge; the other two dragged after it. There was something very frightening about Aunt Sally.

'I shall pinch you if you disobey me, Worzel.'

'Ow!' screamed Gummidge, as Aunt Sally's fingers reached his arm.

'Will you obey me now?' she asked.

'Yes, Aunt,' said Gummidge, flushing a deep brown with terror.

Aunt Sally tweaked Gummidge's hat off his head; then she removed her own bonnet and tied the strings under her nephew's chin. 'Take off your overall,' she said, 'and give it to me.'

Very, very slowly Gummidge pulled off his overall. Aunt Sally took it from his hand. Then she jerked herself behind a holly bush and there was silence for a moment. Gummidge looked very strange in his shirt and trousers. Bits of straw stuck up all round his neck.

Brisk, crackling noises came from behind the

bush, and presently Aunt Sally appeared. She was wearing Gummidge's smock and she held out the clean dress.

'Are your hands clean, Worzel?' she asked.

Gummidge stretched out his fingers and looked at them.

'You can still see the shape of 'em,' he replied slowly. 'My thumbs is a bit earthed-up, but you can see the shape all right.'

Susan looked at them. 'There are bits of straw between your fingers,' she remarked.

'Ooh aye!' agreed Gummidge. 'That's where the mud caked when the dry weather came.'

'You ought to be ashamed of yourself,' said Aunt Sally. 'I have a very good mind not to let you wear my nice clean dress.'

'I don't want to wear your dress,' shouted Gummidge defiantly. 'I'm not a lass. I'm a cock-scarecrow.'

Aunt Sally took no notice, but hustled him into the frock.

'Why is she doing that?' whispered Susan.

'I've got to take her place at the fair,' breathed Gummidge huskily. 'I've got to stand and have things throwed at me. I'd rather be put through the turnip-cutter any day.'

'I think it's a shame,' cried Susan indignantly.

Aunt Sally turned towards her furiously. 'If

you were my little girl, I should send you to bed for the day.'

'Have you got a bed?' asked Susan.

'Ooh aye! She sleeps in a box with the skittles,' whispered Gummidge. He was dressed by now and looked very curious indeed.

'Sit down,' said Aunt Sally to Susan. She was so very severe that Susan obeyed at once, and John also sat down beside her.

'Now go and take my place at the Fair, Worzel,' said Aunt Sally. 'And do not let me see you again for an hour.'

Worzel Gummidge set slowly off in the direction of the village. The children wanted to follow, but every time they moved Aunt Sally snapped, 'Don't fidget.'

Susan felt that she was in the middle of a very bad dream indeed as she watched Gummidge trailing in and out of the trees. When he was out of sight Aunt Sally once more tipped herself backwards against a tree trunk and slithered downwards until she was sitting on the ground.

'You may tell me when an hour has passed by,' she remarked.

'We haven't watches,' replied John.

'There are sixty seconds to the minute,' said Aunt Sally. 'And there are sixty minutes to the hour. You must take it in turns to count loud.

Speak very slowly and distinctly.' She leaned her head against the bush and closed her eyelids with her stiff fingers.

At first the counting was rather fun, because the children felt that they were at the beginning of a very exciting game of hide-and-seek. But by the time they had counted ten minutes and fifty-five seconds they began to feel very tired. Every time they paused Aunt Sally opened an eye with her stiff fingers, and glared at them.

'Fifty-six,' said John.

'Fifty-seven,' said Susan.

'Karrk!' snored Aunt Sally.

'Fifty-eight,' said John.

'KARRK!' snored Aunt Sally.

'Fifty—Come on!' said Susan, and they tip-toed away. When they were safely behind the holly bush they waited for a moment.

'Karrk! Karrk! Karrk!' snored Aunt Sally.

'She can go on counting for herself now,' chuckled John.

'The horrid, horrid thing,' said Susan.

Then they turned and ran between the trees and across the fields until they stopped on the common just opposite to Aunt Sally's canvas screen.

Chapter 11

With his back to the screen, and with a clay pipe in his mouth, stood Worzel Gummidge. The children could see from his face that he had fallen into a deep sulk. A short fat man was sitting at a stool beside a table, which was covered with gold and red and green and purple vases.

'Three shots for a penny,' he wheezed. 'Three shots for a penny only. Walk up, ladies and gentlemen!'

The postman pushed his way through the

crowd and held out a coin to the fat man. 'I'll take sixpennorth,' he said.

Then he walked to the barrier and flung a stick at Gummidge.

Susan shivered, and clutched John by the arm.

'I do think it's a very cruel game,' she said.

The first stick whistled past Gummidge's head, the second just missed his arm, and the third one hit him hard on the shoulder. A furious expression came over his face, and the children noticed that the pale-green flush of temper was slowly deepening in his cheeks.

'Can't we *do* anything?' asked Susan as the fourth stick flapped against the canvas screen.

The postman sent another stick with all his force. This one grazed Gummidge's chin, and then fell into the gaping pocket of the chintz dress.

Susan felt raindrops pattering on to her face as the postman hurled another stick. The rain fell faster and faster; soon there was a perfect deluge. The fat man began to gather up his vases and to hustle them into a tent. The crowd scattered and ran for shelter, but still the postman continued to throw sticks. It was difficult to see Gummidge clearly through the driving rain, but the children were almost certain that they saw him take the stick out of his pocket.

An instant later two sticks whizzed through the air. One hit Gummidge in the leg and the other struck the postman full in the face. Gummidge really had lost his temper at last.

'Who did that?' asked the postman furiously, but nobody answered him, for the crowd had gone away.

'Who did that?' repeated the postman.

'Mebbe the stick hit the tent pole and bounced back at you, Mister,' said the fat man. Just at that moment a second stick hurtled across from the tent and hit the postman.

'I wasn't throwing *then*,' he said sulkily as he shook his bruised hand. 'There's some hanky-panky about that Aunt Sally.'

The fat man raised his voice angrily, and while he was shouting at the postman the children saw Gummidge fall flat on his face and wriggle towards the canvas screen. Then he slipped underneath it. The fat man and the postman were far too busy quarrelling to notice what had happened.

Curious rattly and scratchy noises sounded from behind the screen.

'We'd better go,' whispered Susan. She didn't know why she felt so anxious about Gummidge, who had never been particularly interested in her doings, but she simply couldn't help being fond of him.

The two children slipped past the fat man, and ran behind the screen. Gummidge was nowhere to be seen, but they guessed he must be hiding in a big rubbish pit that had been newly dug by the Fair people. The pit was filled with straw and paper and packing-cases, with here and there an old tin. The rain continued to beat down; it rattled on the tins, and fell with a dull patter on the cardboard boxes.

'He must be there!' said John, and, as he spoke, a piece of old matting began to move, and presently Gummidge's face peeped up at them.

'Don't tell on me!' he begged. 'Cover me up quick, before Aunt sees me!'

'You can't stay there,' whispered Susan. 'It's a most disgusting place to hide in.'

' 'Tain't disgustin'!' said Gummidge. 'I've just found a tin with a nice bit of treacle in it.'

The postman shouted angrily from the other side of the tent. 'I'll have the law on you. You must have thrown those sticks.'

'I didn't,' replied the voice of the fat man. 'Why, where's the Aunt Sally got to?'

Gummidge burrowed down underneath the rubbish. Susan covered him up with the piece of sacking.

'Come on!' whispered John, and they ran across the common together.

They didn't feel that it would be safe for them to stay at the Fair any longer, in case they were questioned about Gummidge. Besides, they were drenched with rain.

'I do hope he'll be all right,' panted Susan as she followed John up the village street. 'He has chosen a terribly messy place to hide in. He is *so* dirty, but I'm getting very fond of him.' They happened to be passing Mrs Kibbins's house as she spoke. They had felt rather shy of it ever since John had pulled up the one groundsel root, so they weren't particularly pleased when Emily Goodenough ran out of the gate and called to them to come and shelter from the rain.

Mrs Kibbins's kitchen was full of neighbours. Mrs Briggs, the washerwoman, was there; so was the policeman's wife. Emmeline, who was now an ordinarily dressed baby, lay in a laundry basket in front of the fire. A stranger, whose name was Mrs Biggledore, was sitting in the only rocking-chair.

The children felt that they wanted to be neither seen nor heard. They were terribly afraid that questions might be asked about Gummidge. However, nobody took much notice of them, and so they were able to sit on the polished fender. while the moisture steamed off their clothes.

'I don't know what Scatterbrook's coming to,'

said the policeman's wife. 'It isn't the place it used to be.'

'It seems good enough, as places go,' remarked Mrs Biggledore. 'We've done quite well out of our Aunt Sally in Scatterbrook. We're going to have it painted tomorrow. I'm making a new bonnet for it now.' She stitched rapidly at a piece of coarse muslin.

Susan looked at John, but he was in a provoking mood, and pretended not to have heard anything.

'I don't hold with Aunt Sallys,' said Mrs Kibbins. 'I think they teach children to be rough. All that stick-throwing can't be good for them. And talking of Aunt Sallys, I can't think where that scarecrow of mine went to. It clean disappeared the day before Emmeline's clothes were changed.'

'Mebbe the gypsies took it,' suggested the washerwoman. 'There've been queer goings on lately. It all began the day my washing was taken. Not that I'd have minded if it hadn't been for Mrs Bloomsbury-Barton's new chemises.'

She looked rather accusingly at John and Susan, who went very red indeed.

Then Emily Goodenough, who noticed their blushes, asked curiously, 'Do you two know where Mrs Kibbins's scarecrow is?'

Susan bit her lips.

142

'Not now,' said John hastily. This was quite true, he felt, for it wasn't to be expected that Gummidge would stay on the rubbish heap.

'Did you *ever* know?' asked Emily Goodenough.

The next questions might have been very awkward indeed for the children if Mrs Kibbins had not jumped up at the sound of a loud knock on her front door.

The children heard her talking, and presently she came into the kitchen again, and said, 'You're wanted, Mrs Biggledore.'

The fat man from the Aunt Sally stand followed her into the room.

'You'd best come home,' he said. 'I'll want you to help me fix the Aunt Sally.'

'Her bonnet isn't finished, Alf,' replied Mrs Biggledore.

'It's a new dress she'll be needing,' replied Mr Biggledore. 'A new dress and a new face. I can't get over it.' He sat down heavily on a very small stool.

'What's the matter, Mr Biggledore?' asked the washerwoman.

'Matter!' he grunted. 'There's a deal the matter. The postman had been having a throw at the Aunt Sally and he turned nasty because he said one of the sticks had bounced back again and hit him.'

'You don't say!' exclaimed Mrs Biggledore. 'That's never happened before.'

'Well,' continued Mr Biggledore. 'Well, not wanting any ill-feeling, I took the postman into the Bat and Belfry and gave him a glass of beer. When I came out again what do you think I saw?' He looked enquiringly round the room.

'Couldn't say,' retorted Mrs Biggledore. 'But I've known you see queer things on the wrong side of an inn door.'

'I saw,' said Mr Biggledore, crossly, 'I saw a great, soft cow running about the common, and what do you think she had on her horns?'

'Mice, most likely,' snapped Mrs Biggledore.

'She'd our Aunt Sally hanging by her skirts. You never saw such a sight. The paint was rubbed off her face, and one leg was broken.'

'You don't say,' gasped Mrs Biggledore.

'I *am* glad!' whispered Susan to John.

'And that's not all,' went on Mr Biggledore. 'Aunt Sally was wearing different clothes from the ones she usually does.'

'You're not right in the head, you know,' said Mrs Biggledore, and all the women gazed at the showman.

'I tell you she were,' he shouted. 'She were wearing an old blue smock.'

'I don't know what's come over Scatterbrook,'

wailed the washerwoman. 'There never used to be goings on like this.'

John and Susan tried hard not to laugh, but it was difficult to keep their mouths from curling up at the corners. They wanted to know how the cow had found Aunt Sally.

'I'll show you,' said Mr Biggledore. He fumbled in a string bag that he carried, and presently he pulled out a tattered blue overall, which he handed to Mrs Biggledore. 'Our Aunt Sally never had anything like that before,' she agreed.

'It's mine,' gasped Mrs Kibbins. 'It's my overall; the one I'd left in the wash-house the day before Emmeline's clothes were changed. I know it by the patch on the sleeve!' She snatched it from Mr Biggledore. 'See, it's got my name on the collar.'

Now unluckily John simply couldn't help winking at Susan. It was so exciting to know more than all the grown-up people, that he had to show off about it. Mrs Kibbins saw the wink.

'I believe you children are at the bottom of this,' she announced.

Mr Biggledore looked at them. Susan and John felt that it was horrid to be stared at by anyone so fat as Mr Biggledore. They shuffled their feet and twiddled with the sleeves of their jerseys.

'Come to think of it,' said Mr Biggledore slowly. 'Come to think of it, they *were* hanging about while I was talking to the postman. That's queer, that is.'

'Have you been meddling with the Aunt Sally?' asked Mrs Biggledore.

'Oh no!' replied Susan, and John added, 'We wouldn't meddle with her for anything in the world.'

'I'm not so sure,' said Mrs Kibbins nastily.

'My goodness gracious!' cried Emily Goodenough. 'It's four o'clock and the sun's shining. Whatever will Mrs Braithewaite say to me for being so late. We must put our best feet foremost.' She stood up, and held out her hands to the children.

Never had John and Susan felt so grateful to anyone. They forgave Emily Goodenough for her cold knobbly fingers, and all her fussiness, as they said goodbye to Mrs Kibbins.

'Oh, *thank* you, Emily,' said Susan as they reached the little garden door.

'Why!' asked Emily, and then added, 'No, don't you tell me, Miss Susan. I can guess.'

But whether she really guessed or not, neither John nor Susan ever knew.

Chapter 12

Susan had caught a chill at the Fair, and so she was not allowed to go out the next day, and Emily kept John in too, because she said it was 'best to be on the safe side.' So, though the day was bright and shining, and all kinds of exciting noises from the farmyard came in through the windows, the children had to play halma, and paint, and make shuttlecocks out of corks and feathers.

Mr Braithewaite had lighted the parlour fire for them, so whenever Emily was out of the room they were able to talk about Gummidge in a way they couldn't have done in the kitchen, where people were constantly bustling in and out.

'I do hope they won't bury that rubbish behind the Aunt Sally stand,' said Susan. 'It would be dreadful if they buried poor Gummidge. He does lead a dangerous sort of life.'

'It would be much worse if he were put into the skittle box with Aunt Sally,' yawned John. 'She'd pinch him all night.'

'We ought to go and look after him,' said Susan, as she stuck the last feather into her cork. 'He's not the sort of person who ought to be left alone.'

But though they begged and pleaded, Emily refused to let them go out. The most she would do for them was to bake them a dough-man with curranty eyes. On any ordinary day they would have loved him, but his stiff arms and legs and round head reminded them so much of Gummidge that they were quite glad when the last crumb was eaten.

To make things worse, the next day was a wet one, and so they were kept indoors again. They sat listening to the rain and longing to hear the sound of Gummidge's jerky footsteps.

'I'm sure if he *is* all right he'll come and see us,' said Susan. But Gummidge did not come.

By Wednesday, when the children were allowed to go out, all the tents and gypsy vans had disappeared from the common, and only a few rags and bits of paper were left to remind people of the visit.

They found a few scraps of orange peel scattered about by the side of Aunt Sally's holly bush, but though they hunted everywhere they could not see a sign of Gummidge.

Presently they went to play in a little copse by the edge of the common.

'We'll never find him now,' sighed Susan. 'I expect Aunt Sally has taken him away with her.'

Just at that moment, something hard flipped down on to John's nose, and then fell to the ground.

'It's a boot button!' he exclaimed, as he stooped to pick it up. 'That's a funny thing to drop out of a tree.'

The children were standing underneath an oak. Its great trunk was scored in several places by lightning, and several of the branches had been torn away.

'What a good tree to climb,' said Susan.

'Umm,' said John. He dug his toe into one of the cracks and tried to hoist himself up. 'Better try the other side,' he said at last.

'There's a "Trespassers will be Prosecuted"

notice board here,' cried Susan. 'What a funny thing to find against a tree.'

The pole of the notice board was a great help to them. They slanted it against the trunk and wriggled along it. Then John managed to haul himself up on to the lowest branch of the tree.

'It's a *hollow* tree!' he cried excitedly. 'There's something sticking up from the inside. Good gracious! It's Gummidge!'

Worzel Gummidge's head and shoulders were sticking up from the middle of the hollow trunk. His cheeks, chin, and forehead were smeared with mud.

'Good morning!' said John, and Susan peeped over his arm. Gummidge stared at them in the most curious manner. His face looked anxious and obstinate. The children could see that he was not sulking, but only terribly in earnest about something.

'Good morning!' said Susan.

Gummidge stared at her; then he settled himself deeper down into the hollow of the tree. Curious oddments were sticking up all around him. The children could see the frayed edge of a piece of linoleum and the end of a rather dashed ostrich feather. Aunt Sally's bonnet was hanging from a twig just above his head.

'You might answer us!' said Susan crossly.

'Ker!' said Gummidge unexpectedly. 'Ker! Ker! Ker!'

'Are you ill?' asked John.

'Ker!' repeated Gummidge. He sounded like a broody hen.

Susan sat astride one of the branches, and stared at the scarecrow.

'We've been looking for you,' she announced.

'Ker! Ker! Ker! KER!' Gummidge sounded very angry. 'Go away! I'm busy. Can't you read notices?'

'What notices?'

'My notice, o' course—the one that says "Trespassers will be Persecuted".'

'You should say *Prosecuted*, not *Persecuted*!' corrected Susan.

'You can say what you like an' I'll say what I like. Go away! I'm busy sitting.' Gummidge shook his head angrily.

'What are you sitting on?' asked Susan.

'Three china eggs and one cardboard Easter one. I'm broody, I am; an' I didn't ought to be disturbed.'

'Don't be silly!' said John. 'Where did the china eggs come from?'

'I got 'em out of Mrs Kibbins's hen-house.'

'But they won't hatch.'

'That's all you know,' snapped Gummidge.

'They won't hatch under hens, because hens is so terrible impatient and only sits three weeks. I'll sit three years if I've a mind to. Why I've stood in the same field for over a year at a time. And sitting's a lot easier than standing.'

'What shall you do with the chickens when they hatch?' asked Susan.

'They mightn't be chickens,' replied Gummidge. 'You never know what might come out of a china egg. I've seen a lot of queer things come out of eggs as well as birds—spiders and frogs and ants and all sorts.'

He ducked his head down with the curious tucking-in movement that reminded Susan of mother hens' movements.

'It took me a time to make the nest, I can tell you,' went on Gummidge. 'I dursen't come out of the rubbish pit except at night, for fear of Aunt Sally.'

'What happened to her?' asked John. 'Did a cow really toss her?'

'The cow happened to be passing the rubbish pit,' said Gummidge. 'So I called out to her, and I said, "You go and fetch Aunt Sally here. She's in the spinney and you'll know her by the smell of turnip on her clothes. You go and fetch her here and treat her rough on the way." Well, the cow hadn't anything particular to do; besides, she had an aunt of her own, so she was always willing to treat one roughly. Off she galloped, and presently she came back with Aunt Sally dangling from her horns. I like that cow.'

'Was Aunt Sally much hurt?' asked Susan.

'Well she was a bit bashed about,' admitted Gummidge. 'Her hair had come off and her nose was chipped. I laughed till my stuffing rustled when I saw Aunt Sally trying to pinch the cow's horns. Then Mr Biggledore knocked her off with a broom and took her into the tent.'

'Where were you?' asked Susan.

'I were in the rubbish tip, and I heard it all. They painted her next day. There's a fly on her nose that will stay there for ever.'

'Why?' asked John.

'It stuck there when the paint was wet,' wheezed Gummidge. 'So now she'll have a tickle on her nose for ever and ever.'

'Has she left Scatterbrook now?' asked Susan.

'Yes, they packed her in the skittle box and took her away with them. I know that for I was collecting bits of stuff for the nest when the van went away.'

Susan was just wondering how Gummidge had managed to escape being seen, when he continued: 'I was disguised as a bramble bush with little bits of newspaper tangled in the branches. And then the moon was kind; she never peeped but once, so other folks couldn't see neither. Anyway, they'd probably have mistaken my face for a bird's nest; it looks quite nice and mossy still, doesn't it?'

'Don't you ever wash it?' asked John.

'Not o' purpose! Sometimes the rain washes it for me. I like a bit of variety in a face myself. Once a hay-seed rooted in my eyebrow, and it sprung up as strong as anything. It was a fine sight by hay-harvest.'

'I think,' said Susan primly, 'I think it's rather untidy to grow things on faces.'

Gummidge looked offended, and closed his eyes. As he continued to sit in silence for some time, the children began to scramble about on the branches of the tree.

Presently they heard Gummidge's voice raised miserably, 'I don't know what to do about it. No, I don't!'

'What's the matter now?' asked Susan.

'The robin's the matter. The nest is still in my coat pocket, and the eggs is due to hatch out.'

'Where's your coat then?' asked John.

'I left it on a heap o' pea-sticks in Mrs Kibbins's garden. It does seem a thing to think of the eggs hatching out among strangers, but I daren't leave my own nest.' He looked doubtfully at Susan, and then said, 'You see, the eggs'll take cold if I leave them. I suppose you wouldn't care to sit for a bit, while I go and fetch the coat.'

'No, I wouldn't,' said Susan, who didn't happen to feel in the mood for sitting still.

'Oh dear!' said Gummidge. Tears trickled down his nose, and sparkled like dew on the green tufts of mildew. He looked very miserable indeed.

'I wonder if we could get the coat,' said Susan, who couldn't bear to see the scarecrow in tears. She looked at John, but he shook his head.

'I don't think Mrs Kibbins likes us very much,' he said. 'And I don't think we could get into her garden without being seen.'

'You could at night,' said Gummidge. 'You could disguise yourselves as rubbish heaps or something. Do now! and we'll have a lovely hatching out in the morning. The eggs are due to chip today. I'll give you a present if you'll fetch the coat.'

'What will you give us?' asked John.

'That'd be telling,' said Gummidge. 'Ooh aye, that'd be telling. And now you mustn't disturb me any more. Good morning.'

He closed his eyes once more, and ruffled the sleeves of his chintz frock with a most curious bird-like movement. The children waited for some time, but as he didn't speak again, they scrambled down from the tree and left him sitting there. He looked very queer in his chintz dress.

Chapter 13

They passed Mrs Kibbins's cottage on their way back to the farm, and when they looked over the hedge, they saw that Gummidge's coat was still hanging on the heap of pea-sticks. Far above them, on the topmost spray of a pear tree, perched Father Robin, who was singing very wildly indeed.

'Can't we get the coat now?' asked Susan. But she knew, as she spoke, that it would be impossible, for Mrs Kibbins's head showed above the row of geranium pots in the window.

When they went into the farm kitchen, they saw

that a stranger was standing by the open doorway. He was a queer little bent-up man, dressed in an old velveteen coat and breeches. He was talking to Mrs Braithewaite in a thin, high voice.

'I saw your scarecrow was gone,' he said. 'And I thought mebbe as how——'

'The master can make another for himself as easy as not,' interrupted Mrs Braithewaite. 'We don't need to pay to have an old face carved out of a turnip.'

'There's luck in tatie bogles,' replied the old man. 'Some of them are queer and some are lucky, and some are no use at all. I've been making them for fifty years, and I should know something about them. I made the one that stood in Ten-acre field about twelve months ago, when I was hedging and ditching.'

'I don't waste time in talking,' said Mrs Braithewaite snappily.

The old man looked at her in rather a queer way, before he turned round and tramped down the cobbled path.

Susan and John ran through the side door and met him at the gate.

'Did you make Mr Worzel Gummidge?' asked Susan shyly. The old man looked at her mysteriously. Susan noticed that his eyes were as bright as a robin's.

'I made the scarecrow that used to stand in Ten-acre field,' he admitted.

'Did you know that he was really alive?' she asked.

'Why shouldn't he be alive?' replied the old man. 'He was made out of a good live turnip. There's bad turnips and good turnips, but the slow growers is the best. I reckon the farmer had better be careful if he means to make a scarecrow himself. I've made 'em for the farmers round about for over fifty years and I've always been careful to choose kindly roots. Where's the old scarecrow got to?'

'He's in an oak tree in the spinney, by Ten-acre field,' said John. 'He's pretending to be a bird.'

'They will have their fancies,' said the old man. Then he shouldered his pack again, and walked down the lane.

The children felt rather glad to know that there was at least one person in Scatterbrook who believed what they said about Worzel Gummidge.

But they did not have much time in which to think about the old man; they were too busy making plans for the evening's adventure. It was decided that John should keep awake until ten o'clock and that Susan should keep watch after that.

At last bedtime came, and they went upstairs.

From her window Susan could see Farmer Braithewaite at work in one of the outhouses. He appeared to be filling a sack with straw. Every now and then he crossed the yard to the kitchen and then stumped back again. Usually he went to bed at nine o'clock.

'You're never going to Ten-acre tonight?' called Mrs Braithewaite from the kitchen.

'Yes, I am,' replied the farmer.

John felt rather troubled. He was dreadfully afraid that Gummidge might leave his nest and go for a walk in his old field and so meet the farmer. As he was thinking about this, the yard door shut with a bang, and he guessed that the farmer had gone. It was half-past nine before John heard the sound of his returning boots. There followed the noise of jarring bolts and snecking window-catches, as the farmer and his wife made the house safe for the night.

After that Susan kept watch until eleven o'clock, when she roused John.

The whole house seemed restless; boards creaked as the children set foot on the stairways, and the doors, however carefully they might be unlatched, yawned loudly like fitful sleepers half aroused from dreams. Every clock seemed determined to sound the alarm, so loud was its ticking.

At last, however, the front door bolt rasped

back into its socket, the last dying squeak of the hinges wore itself out, and the children stood safely in the little porch and looked about them.

They had never been out and alone in the night before, and for a minute or two they waited while the shadows slipped along the garden wall.

'Come on,' said John, a little breathlessly, and he took Susan's hand.

The hedges on either side of the lane seemed to have thickened during the night; the bushes seemed larger, fuzzier, and more important. If it had not been for the friendly rustlings of birds among the twigs, Susan might have been frightened. John was rather scared.

But when they reached the village they felt quite adventurous again. It was fun to be out in the night and to see above the familiar walls little pairs of drawn blinds—the closed eyelids of the houses.

'I expect Mrs Kibbins looks funny in bed!' whispered John.

'I'm glad she doesn't know we're here,' said Susan. 'Isn't it lovely to think that nobody in the world knows that we are here, unless Gummidge has guessed.'

They opened Mrs Kibbins's gate and then tiptoed down the garden path till they reached the patch of earth. Docks and groundsel brushed wet leaves against their legs, and the earth felt sticky beneath their feet, as they walked to the pile of pea-sticks.

'It's still here,' whispered John. Then, very, very gently, so as not to disturb Mrs Robin, he lifted the coat from a forked stick.

'It's absolutely sodden,' whispered Susan, as she felt the damp coat. 'I do hope the robin babies are safe still inside the eggs. It would be dreadful to be hatched with rheumatism.'

'I wonder if we shall hear the eggs chipping,' said John. 'It's so still tonight that we might hear anything.'

'Come on!' said Susan, who was afraid of Mrs Kibbins waking up. And they hurried away.

'I hope Gummidge won't interfere with the eggs,' said John as they walked up the village street again. 'I hope he won't want to open them before they are ready. He is so awfully impatient, and he might look rather frightening to a newly hatched robin.'

'Especially to one that wasn't used to scarecrows,' added Susan.

'You can't be used to scarecrows when you are inside an egg,' argued John. 'You can't even have heard about them.'

'Not unless Mrs Robin has shouted to them through the cracks,' said Susan.

They walked on in silence then until they came to the corner of Ten-acre field.

'Why, there's Gummidge,' cried Susan.

A familiar-looking figure was flapping tattered coatsleeves in the middle of Ten-acre field. A little breeze had set up, and the scarecrow seemed to be moving more briskly than usual.

'Let's creep up behind him, and surprise him,' whispered John. So they picked their way as quickly as possible over the long furrows. Soon they stood exactly behind the scarecrow.

'Boo!' said Susan, but there was no reply.

'I suppose he's sulking as usual,' said John.

'Look what we've brought you,' he added, and he ran round to the front of the scarecrow.

But the face that stared out at him from under the old cap was not Worzel Gummidge's. It belonged to a new and very stupid-looking scarecrow, who had a sharp nose and no knobbles, and a foolishly grinning mouth.

'It—it isn't Gummidge at all,' said John as he backed away from the creature.

'Then whoever is it?' asked Susan, in a horrified whisper, as she crept closer to the creature.

'Who are you!' asked John.

There was no reply, and the strange scarecrow did not so much as blink an eyelid. His face was clean and polished, and rather yellow. Instead of hands, two spade-handles stuck out from his coat sleeves. He was fatter than Worzel Gummidge, and looked very much tidier.

'How perfectly awful,' said Susan. 'Do you think he can have killed our dear Gummidge?'

A noisy creak answered her, as the wind whistled round the scarecrow and swung him slightly sideways.

'Why! He hasn't even got legs,' shouted John. 'He's just stuck on to a post. He hasn't anything but a long coat—not trousers nor a waistcoat nor braces nor anything. He couldn't walk if he wanted to.'

'He might hop, though,' suggested Susan in a terrified whisper. 'I don't like him at all. He's got a horrid, horrid face. Let's come away. I'm afraid of him hopping after us. I'd simply *hate* to be hopped after.'

She turned away and began to walk towards the spinney.

'I know he's going to hop after us,' she gasped.

'After all lots of birds *do* hop,' said John, who felt a little scared himself. 'Lots of birds always hop when they are on the ground.'

'But they only do it for swank,' said Susan. 'They only do it to show that they can. A scarecrow with a broomstick leg might hop so terribly high.'

She scrambled over the hedge that bordered the spinney and ran to Gummidge's oak tree.

'Gummidge!' called Susan.

There was a dead silence.

'Gummidge,' said Susan again, and then she began to scramble up the slanting notice-board. She had never climbed so quickly in all her life. John followed more slowly; he was afraid of crushing the nest in the coat pocket.

'Gummidge,' said Susan desperately, as she reached the branch that was level with Gummidge's nest.

A noisy rustling answered her.

'Shoo!' said Gummidge suddenly. 'Shoo! Shoo! Shoo!' He popped up his head and then raised a stiff arm from the nest and slowly raised his closed eyelids.

'Shoo!' he repeated sleepily.

Susan nearly fell off the branches because his shooing was so gusty and she was so frightened.

'Oh! it's you,' said Gummidge sleepily. 'I'd just been dreaming about those pesky crows.'

'We've brought your coat back,' said John.

'I'm much obliged to be sure,' muttered Gummidge. 'You'd best hang it on a twig. I won't put it on until the morning.' He closed his eyes again, and burrowed down into the nest.

'You *must* wake up,' said Susan. 'You simply

mustn't go to sleep again, a most dreadful thing has happened.'

'Eh?' said Gummidge.

Then John took up the tale, and continued, 'There's another scarecrow in the middle of Ten-acre. He's standing in your old place, and he wouldn't speak to us. He's only got one leg.'

'And quite enough too for the likes of him,' snapped Gummidge. 'You've got to learn to think quickly when you've got two legs, or else you'll find yourself stepping with both at once or the same one always. It took me a while to learn.'

'Is he a relation?' asked Susan, who simply couldn't understand why Gummidge showed no surprise.

'Relation!' jeered Gummidge. 'Relation indeed! He's only a common Swede. We Mangold Worzels don't mix with the Swedes. I know all about them.'

'How did you know that the other scarecrow was there?' asked John.

'Friend of mine happened to be passing,' said Gummidge carelessly. 'I saw an old friend tonight—the one who throwed me together and cut my face out. He told me. But I'll scare the other Bogle out of the field tomorrow. I'm going to sleep now.'

'But what about us?' asked Susan miserably. 'I

can't go back through Ten-acre. I'm afraid of that Swedish scarecrow. I'm very frightened.'

'There now,' said Gummidge soothingly. 'You come in here along of me, and you'll be all right.'

He moved to one side of the nest and made room for John and Susan. 'It's all right,' he said. 'I knows how to look after children all right. I sorted out the nest this morning and it's fit for a robin to nest in.'

Susan scrambled down into the knobbly hollow of the oak tree and John followed her. A sharp scent of turnip was blended with the warm, tickly smell of dry hay.

Susan sniffed. 'It smells like a greengrocer's shop,' she murmured.

Gummidge tucked a piece of dry sacking round them and made a curious crooning sound until they fell asleep.

Chapter 14

Afterwards, when Susan lay in her own bed, and listened to the clinking of the milk-pails in the farmyard, she found it difficult to remember the happenings of the night before. Bees droned in and out of the window, and flopped heavily against the panes. The sound of their buzzing reminded her of something and then she remembered that they sounded rather like Gummidge's crooning voice.

She remembered being awakened by the scarecrow very early in the morning, when the tops of the hedges were all blurred and fuzzy with mist. And she remembered a strange, cool walk across Ten-acre field, with Gummidge on one side of her and John on the other. The scarecrow had left them at the farmhouse door, and then they had tiptoed upstairs to bed.

While she was wondering if the young robins had hatched, and if anything exciting had come out of Gummidge's china eggs, Emily Goodenough clattered into the room, and said 'Time to get up, Miss Susan' in her most everyday voice.

It was very difficult indeed to get up, but at last Susan rubbed the sleep out of her eyes and tumbled out of bed.

After breakfast, Susan and John scurried away to Ten-acre field. The strange scarecrow was still there, and opposite to him, with its pole planted well down into the earth and its board on a level with his stupid eyes, stood Worzel Gummidge's notice-board. The children stopped to read the words 'Trespassers will be Prosecuted'.

But the scarecrow was not the only occupant of the field, for mincing up and down among the furrows, pecking here, there, and everywhere, was a vast company of rooks. The children had never seen so many before. One of them was perched on the scarecrow's head and was pecking thoughtfully at his neck. Another very raggedy one balanced himself on the notice-board and croaked impertinently at the scarecrow.

Some of the crows lifted, as John and Susan approached them, flapped slow wings, and settled down to breakfast at the other end of the field. Others continued to swagger up and down the furrows.

'Let's go and look for Gummidge!' said John.

At the entrance to the spinney, they were met by Worzel Gummidge himself. He was wearing his old coat, and Father Robin was singing happily on the top of his sun-bonnet. It was just like old times.

'Good morning,' said Gummidge. 'We've had a lovely hatch. There's four of 'em in here.' He patted the pocket of his coat, then snatched at a passing gnat and handed it to Mrs Robin, who darted her head out of the pocket and snapped swiftly.

'Oh! May we look at them?' asked Susan.

'No, you can't,' said Gummidge. 'Young birds have a right to choose their own friends.'

'Wife! Wife!' sang Mr Robin proudly, and he zipped across to a bramble spray.

Then Susan remembered Gummidge's promise.

'You promised you'd give us a present if we brought back the coat,' she said.

'And so I have,' said Gummidge sulkily. 'I've given you four real nice robins.'

'But you won't let us look at them,' objected John.

'There's lots of things belong to you that you can never look at,' said Gummidge. 'You can't look at your own face.'

'What about looking-glasses?' asked Susan.

Gummidge didn't reply, but then he may never have heard about looking-glasses. 'You can't look at your tempers or the insides of your heads, neither, and *they* belongs to you.'

'Well, can't we take the robins home with us?' asked John, who had been listening rather impatiently.

Gummidge only stared at him, and muttered, 'Don't talk so soft!'

Presently he said, 'I'm tired of humans!' and, swinging round angrily, he began to walk into Ten-acre field.

'Them Swedes has no idea of keeping themselves to themselves,' he complained. 'Fancy making friends with rooks—great common birds that build their nests about in the sight of anyone. Great ugly gawks that come out of splodgy eggs. I've no patience with them.'

He sat down by the hedge, and took his clay pipe out of his pocket.

'I've given that Swede notice that I'll persecute him if he doesn't clear out of my field. Ooh aye. If he's not read my notice by tonight I'll learn him!' remarked Gummidge fiercely. 'And he won't forget it in a hurry. I'm giving a party tonight.'

'What sort of a party?' asked Susan.

'A party of scarecrows, o' course. I've been sending messages to all the ones that live hereabouts. The Bogles is coming and the Mangold-Worzels. It's a pity it's the wrong time o' year for the Snows.'

'The Snows?' said John, in a puzzled voice.

'The Snow Men. But anyway they're too shy for parties. Shy and moody, that's what they are! They'll melt to nothing as soon as look at you. I remember on my last birthday—'

'When was your last birthday?' interrupted Susan.

'In December, and I've another today!'

'You can't have two birthdays in one year,' objected John.

'That's all you know!' said Gummidge. 'Some years I has eight or nine. I've one birthday for my head and another for my arms and another for my back, and so on. I used to have a grand birthday for my stummick afore the spadgers stole it.'

'We've only one birthday a year,' sighed Susan, who was beginning to feel it must be lovely to be a scarecrow.

'That's because you're all made out of the same piece,' said Gummidge pityingly. 'Now today's the sixtieth birthday of my legs. Sixty years ago today, my legs were an acorn.'

'How do you know?' asked John.

'Talk gets about,' replied Gummidge.

'Oughtn't we to give him a present?' whispered Susan to John.

Gummidge leaned sideways to listen.

'I'll tell you what I'd like,' he said wistfully. 'I'd like a nice wife.'

Susan looked at him reprovingly. 'That's rather a big thing to ask for,' she told him. 'People who aren't relations generally give handkerchiefs for presents.'

'I've got one o' them. I've got one nearly all the time except when it flies about.' He patted his nest-pocket.

'I know!' said Susan excitedly. 'I know what I'll give you. I've just thought of a lovely present. I'll bring it this afternoon.'

Gummidge looked at her suspiciously.

'It's not a mouse, is it? Granfer Bogle gave me a mouse when I was first put together. She went and built a nest in my boot, and I had to stand still for a fortnight.'

'No, it's not a mouse.'

Gummidge looked happier.

'Not a watch?' he persisted. 'One of the Snows gave me a watch.'

'Did it keep good time?' asked John.

'It did that! The hands stood at twelve o'clock—dinner-time, you know—all day long. But I had to defy it in the end. I got too fat.'

'How do you defy a watch?' asked Susan.

'Same way as you defy anything else, don't take any notice of it. You'd better be off now. I'm going to have a sulk in my nest. The party starts at ten o'clock tonight; you can come if you like.'

Gummidge whistled to Father Robin, who instantly returned to perch on his hat, and John and Susan said goodbye.

They felt so tired after their late night that, directly dinner was over, they went up to the hay-loft and slept all the afternoon.

'We *must* go to that party,' said John, some hours later, as he sat up and shook the hay from his hair.

'Emily won't let us,' said Susan. 'She'd ask all sorts of questions.'

'We'll have to go without asking then,' said John. But Susan wouldn't agree to that. She argued that there are some things you can do and some things you can't, and that it would be really wicked to go to a party without permission.

'If you ask you'll only go and spoil it all,' grumbled John.

When they went back to the house, they found Emily was very busy fitting a new overall on to Mrs Braithewaite. Her mouth was full of pins, and as the dress wasn't behaving very nicely, she scarcely listened to what Susan said.

'May we go—?' began Susan, and just at that moment John upset a box of pins, which hindered Emily but helped the children.

'Go where you like,' she said, 'so long as you're not late for supper.'

'We shan't be late for supper,' explained Susan. 'Because you see we don't want to go till—'

'You're standing on my tape-measure!' said Emily.

'Then may we—?'

'Go where you like and when you like so long as you don't get into mischief and don't keep meals waiting. I never saw such children for fussing.'

'Come on,' said John, and though Susan looked as though she would have liked to explain things to Emily, she followed him out of the kitchen.

Even then she didn't feel quite comfortable about the party, and at supper she began to ask again about the party. Luckily for her and

John, she wasn't able to ask many questions because every time she began Emily who was in a fussy mood told her not to talk so much or not to talk at all with her mouth full or not to interrupt.

It really wasn't Susan's fault that she did not get very special permission to go to Gummidge's birthday party.

The children did not find it difficult to keep awake that night; there was so much to be done before the party. As soon as Emily had been in to say goodnight, which she did earlier than usual, because she was going to see one of her friends in the village, Susan hurried out of bed, and began to look for Gummidge's birthday presents.

She found an old pair of stockings, a darning egg, and the card case that she had bought at the jumble sale.

He'll like the egg, she thought. It will do for his nest, but I hope he won't be disappointed in the other things. Then she remembered her pig money-box, and wrapped that up as well; something that might have been a penny and might have been a halfpenny rattled inside it.

Meanwhile, John had collected a cake of soap, a tube of toothpaste, and a picture postcard of Scatterbrook.

When the big clock on the church steeple

struck ten o'clock, he went into Susan's room, and begged her to hurry up.

Now that they knew the ways of door and staircase, the children did not feel so frightened as they had done the night before.

'After all,' whispered John, on the way past Mrs Braithewaite's bedroom door, 'after all, Emily said we could go, so I don't see how Mrs Braithewaite can stop us, even if she does wake.'

Susan didn't answer until they were safely in the porch.

'I don't think Emily really knew the time of the party. Do you think we ought to go back?'

'Don't be a silly,' said John.

Chapter 15

When they reached the field, they peeped over the hedge rather nervously.

'Why, whatever are those?' whispered Susan. For a moment she thought that the field was full of giant rooks, but when she looked again she saw that the large, flapping things that were stalking over the furrows were scarecrows. There were more than a dozen of them, and they were all walking very queerly indeed.

'That's a very wide one over there,' said John. And then he saw that the two scarecrows, who had only one leg each, had linked their arms and were taking it in turns to hop forward.

Another one, who was evidently not used to walking, picked up one leg in both hands, planted it firmly in front of him, then seized the other leg, and so on.

'It would be dreadful for him if he were in a hurry,' said Susan. She shrank back into the shadow of the hedge as she spoke for a very short, three-legged scarecrow was walking past. No, she was not exactly walking, for she appeared to be entirely jointless, and moved with a curious rolling gait. The children guessed that her legs had once belonged to a milking stool. Her velveteen coat reached the ground, and her sailor hat was much too large for her. It rolled sideways, as she trundled along, now falling over one eye, now over the other. However, she seemed to be a cheerful, determined little creature; every time she fell over, she murmured, 'Upsidaisy, upsidaisy!'

'Do you think we might speak to her, and ask where Gummidge is?' whispered Susan to John. 'She seems quite kind, and I don't like the look of some of the others.'

The small scarecrow rolled over into the hedge as she spoke, and lay there, rolling feebly and muttering, 'Upsidaisy, upsidaisy!'

'Can I help you?' asked Susan, and she held

out her hand. The creature grinned at her, and held out an arm as round as a rolling pin. Its hand was covered with a scratchy woollen glove and, as Susan took it, she could feel paper rustling inside.

'Thank 'ee, my dear,' said the scarecrow. 'And what field do you come from?'

'We don't come from any field,' replied Susan rather indignantly. She didn't like being mistaken for a scarecrow, even though she did love Gummidge.

'One of them new-fangled kind from the allotment gardens, are you?' she said pleasantly. 'Someone must have taken quite a deal of trouble when they cut your face out.'

'It isn't carved,' said Susan.

'Stuffed, is it!' she answered. 'Stuffing's all right in the dry weather, of course, but it does hold water terribly in a wet season.'

Susan felt that it was useless to argue with her, so she changed the subject by saying, 'Do you know where Worzel Gummidge is?'

'I keeps on seeing him, and then I keeps on losing him again, as I turns round,' said the fat scarecrow. 'Last time I looked, he was talking to a lady.'

'What sort of a lady?' asked John.

The little scarecrow dropped her voice. 'A daft

one,' she answered. 'She was dressed by a looney, who used to be a hairdresser. I know her well because I live in the field next to his garden. They say he had a lot like her in his shop in London. She's got a pink wax face and yellow hair, and she wears a blue paper bonnet. But she's a good scarer; not a bird will come near her.'

'I should like to see her,' said Susan.

'There's no mistaking her,' replied the little creature. 'You can come along with me if you like.' She continued to roll oddly along by the side of the hedge; John and Susan walked on beside her. 'I can see you are *jointed*!' she panted presently. 'Can you sit down quite easily?'

'Of course we can,' said John.

'I've always longed to be able to sit,' she sighed. 'Still I mustn't grumble. I've three legs to be thankful for. They say there's going to be a battle tonight,' she continued.

'Who against?' asked Susan.

'We'll have to pick sides before we can tell that,' she replied. 'I hope Mr Gummidge will pick me; I like Mr Gummidge.'

'*She* doesn't,' said a mournful voice just behind them. The children jumped round, and saw Worzel Gummidge himself. Sitting beside him was a large pink waxen lady. She was wearing a pink paper dress, and she was simpering at the reflection of her own face in a mirror that she held. The children had often seen people exactly like her in the windows of the hairdressers' shops. Gummidge was gazing at her in the saddest manner, but the pink lady went on admiring herself, and took not the slightest notice of him.

'Don't you think she's beautiful?' asked Gummidge, and then before anyone could reply, he added, 'She doesn't care for my face.'

'What a shame!' cried Susan.

'I've tried everything,' continued Gummidge. 'I've tried coaxing and petting, and scolding and all sorts. I've even tried kissing.'

The pink wax lady shuddered as he said this.

'Kissing's so difficult,' complained Gummidge. 'I don't seem able to get the time right. Either I kisses before I reach her, or else my mouth slips on her face.'

Susan noticed then that there were a few muddy streaks on the waxen lady's bright pink cheeks.

Suddenly the short, fat scarecrow spoke. 'If you'll excuse me, Mr Gummidge,' she said, 'I don't think that lady is the wife for you. Her face would run in the hot weather.'

'Where to?' asked Gummidge anxiously.

'It would melt.'

'I wouldn't mind *that*,' said Gummidge, with

an affectionate smile. 'I'd always know her by her hair.'

Susan giggled, and John stuffed his handkerchief into his mouth, though Emily Goodenough had often told him that it was a horrid thing to do.

'Won't you marry me?' asked Gummidge, as he turned to the wax lady.

'Oh! Mr Gummidge,' she simpered. 'This is so very sudden.'

'It's a sudden world,' retorted Gummidge, and he flung a stiff arm across her shoulder. The lady moved indignantly away.

'Don't!' she said pettishly.

'I shall if I chooses,' said Gummidge sullenly. 'I'll do what I like with my own arm. You might be marrying me, instead of me marrying you, the way you're going on.'

'I'm not going to marry you,' said the wax lady in a shrill, high voice. 'I'm going to marry a gentleman out of one of the shop windows.'

'Then I hope he'll melt!' shouted Gummidge. 'And if he does, you needn't come worrying me to marry you, for I shan't. Your hair is the colour of a dandelion, and your cheeks are as pink as a worm.'

He stood up as he spoke, and so suddenly that the pink wax lady fell over into the hedge.

Gummidge turned to the children. 'I'm going to talk to that Swede now,' he said.

The scarecrows were still tottering about in the field, tumbling over one another, and making frantic efforts to keep on their legs.

Susan was particularly interested in one lady scarecrow, who wore a cloak of sacking, and who carried a little paper windmill in her hand. Her face was as brown as a potato, and she had bright green hair, sprouting rather low down on her forehead. She had bottle straw boots, and a blue check apron, and she moved hoppingly like a sparrow.

'Good evening, Mr Gummidge,' she said as she hurried up to him. Then she held out the paper windmill. 'For you!' she said simply.

Gummidge beamed at her, took the windmill, and waved it joyfully. 'I've not seen you for a month of Sundays,' he said.

'I'm at Dimden now,' she answered. 'I've a lovely field there.'

'That's a good step away,' said Gummidge.

'But I don't have to step,' said the little creature. 'I've got a bike now.'

She scuttled away to the hedge, and presently returned, dragging a perambulator wheel that was fixed to a long pole. She arranged herself astride it, and began to paddle along with her legs. Really she moved much more slowly than when she was walking, for the wheel sank deeply into the clarty soil, but she seemed to be enjoying herself.

Gummidge looked envious.

'I wish I'd a bike,' he said wistfully. 'Ooh aye! I've often longed for one.'

Then he remembered the children.

'These are my friends,' he said. 'And this,' he waved his arm to the cyclist scarecrow, 'this is Miss Earthy Mangold.'

The children shook hands solemnly. They liked the twiggy feeling of Earthy Mangold's fingers.

'I wish I'd a bike,' repeated Gummidge.

'I'll lend you mine,' said Earthy; she really was a dear little thing.

Then Susan remembered the birthday presents, and she gave Gummidge the stockings, the pig money-box, and the card case, Gummidge snatched them hurriedly, and then he flopped down on to the ground. He seemed to be delighted with the money-box. Earthy Mangold looked so longingly at the stockings and the card case that he threw them at her.

'Wedding present,' he said.

'Whose wedding?' asked Earthy.

'That'd be telling,' muttered Gummidge.

Before Earthy could ask any more questions,

John remembered his presents, and he threw the cake of soap, the toothpaste, and the picture postcard into Gummidge's lap.

'Much obliged, I'm sure,' muttered Worzel, but he was not looking at the presents, he was staring at Earthy Mangold's little brown face. He stared so long that the children thought he must have fallen into one of his sulks, so they hurried away to join a group of scarecrows who were throwing lumps of mud at a smaller one. As soon as the children came near, the scarecrows all stumped away to another corner of the field.

Susan and John wandered away rather disconsolately, until they reached the place where the Swede scarecrow stood. The notice board was still planted in front of him and he looked as foolish as ever.

'They say that's the enemy,' said a little voice, and then the children looked round and saw the three-legged scarecrow. 'The battle is going to begin at cock-crow; that's always the proper time for battles.'

'Shall we be able to fight?' asked John. But before the little creature had time to reply there was a hoarse shout from Gummidge—'Come here! I wants you.'

They ran back to the other side of the field, where they saw a most remarkable sight. Sitting on Gummidge's knee, and lathering his uneven chin with John's new toothpaste, was Earthy Mangold.

Gummidge took the brush out of his mouth, and then said proudly, 'Me and her are going to get married, aren't we, Earthy!'

'Yes, Worzel dear,' replied Earthy shyly.

Gummidge beamed at her.

'May we come and stay with you when you are married?' asked Susan eagerly.

Worzel Gummidge looked puzzled. 'We shan't be staying ourselves,' he said slowly. 'We're going to walk about the world for a bit. You can stay here if you like until we come back—that is, if we do come back.'

'I wouldn't like to stay here with that horrid new scarecrow,' said Susan.

'I'd forgotten all about him,' said Gummidge. 'We've got to have our battle now. Come on, Earthy.'

But the little creature burst into a storm of green tears. 'Don't leave me, Worzel,' she sobbed. 'You might get your face altered before I've got used to it.'

'Do you like my face, duckie?' asked Gummidge tenderly.

'It's a lovely face,' said Earthy. 'And each side's different; that's what I like about it.'

She put up a small hand and patted Gummidge's nose.

'Now you hold my coat, my dear,' said Gummidge. 'You hold my coat, and then the robins won't get spilt. We'll have a lovely walk this evening.'

He took off his coat and handed it to Earthy Mangold, who continued to sob bitterly. Gummidge patted her on the head in a most consoling manner and then, followed by the children, he walked sideways until he stood opposite to the Swede.

Susan looked back and saw that Earthy was riding her bicycle up and down by the hedge side. She was a cheerful little thing and appeared to have forgotten all about the battle.

The other scarecrows crowded round Gummidge, who rooted up the notice-board, and slapped the Swede hard in the face.

'We'll pick up sides,' shouted Gummidge. 'I'll choose the first six because it's my birthday and then you can choose six.'

The Swede continued to smile stupidly.

'I don't think he understands,' said John.

'There's none so deaf as those that won't hear,' retorted Gummidge, and then he roared loudly, 'I choose Clarty, and Singled and Worzel Furrow, and Bulgy and Sprouter and Blight!' Six tall, fierce-looking scarecrows staggered forward and stood in a row. Susan noticed with horror that one of them carried a pitchfork.

'It's your turn now,' shouted Worzel Gummidge.

The Swede smiled quite pleasantly.

'Now, I'm warning you,' said Gummidge, and he shook a knobbly finger. 'I'm warning you. If *you* don't choose, I shall, and then I shall have the biggest army.'

Still the Swede smiled.

'Muddy!' screamed Gummidge. 'Muddy and Rootbound, and Soggy Boggart and Scarer Tater and Rag-bag and Mangoldy.'

Six more scarecrows joined Gummidge's army. One of these was a lady, who wore a basket on her head.

'Your turn again,' said Gummidge to the Swede, but before the other had time to smile, he shouted, 'Ditcher and Bolger and Spring Up! and Yarrow.'

There were only two scarecrows left; one of them was the little Upsidaisy and the other was a lady, whose hair was made of tarred string.

'What's your name?' asked Gummidge.

'Hannah!' replied the lady in a low voice.

'Hannah what?'

'Hannah Harrow,' she replied meekly, and then added, 'I can't fight; the mice have been at me.'

She sagged as she spoke, and flopped emptily to the ground. The children saw that she lay on a small heap of sawdust that had evidently trickled out of her body.

'That's a pity,' said Gummidge. 'Ooh aye! That does seem a pity.' Then he shouted, 'Upsidaisy!'

The three-legged scarecrow rolled towards him, and smiled happily.

'Let's begin the fight,' said Gummidge impatiently.

'It really isn't fair for all of us to fight one scarecrow,' objected John.

'That's all you know about it,' said Gummidge.

A long pause followed, while some of the scarecrows gathered lumps of clay, and others planted their legs deeply down into the ground. And still the Swede stood there and smiled.

'I'm sure he doesn't understand,' said Susan. 'I don't think he's really alive.'

'Of course he's not alive,' said Gummidge. 'He's only a sham scarecrow, a mock Bogle! I wouldn't fight him if he was alive. I'm much too soft-hearted.'

'But if he's dead, he can't fight,' argued John.

'But we're alive and we can,' chirruped Upsidaisy. 'When are you going to begin, Mr Gummidge?'

But Mr Gummidge held up a warning finger, and the scarecrows tottered forward to listen. Susan could hear nothing but the rustling of their bodies and the slow creakings of their limbs. Then suddenly from a distant farm there came a shrill crow, as the earliest rooster sounded the alarm of morning.

Gummidge slapped the Swede in the face. Upsidaisy trundled along and butted him in the middle, another scarecrow wrenched his arm so violently that it came out of his sleeve and fell to the ground. They all flocked round, pulling, tugging and twisting, looking like so many rooks on a newly-sown furrow.

Gummidge stepped back and wiped his forehead. 'Ain't it a lovely battle!' he asked.

Just at that moment, one of the lady scarecrows seized hold of the Swede's head, and jerked it off its pole.

'How very, very horrid,' cried Susan as the head came spinning into her lap. But when she picked it up, she saw that it was only a turnip after all. Certainly the root was carved into the shape of a grinning face, but it was all hard and dried-up. Gummidge was quite right; the Swede was only a mock scarecrow, and had never had a moment's life.

Then John flung himself into the fray, and

knocked the pole over. He picked it up and raced round the field, while all the scarecrows hirpled after him. Soon there was nothing left of the Swede but odd handfuls of straw, a couple of spade-handles, and an old coat; since these were scattered all over the field, it was difficult to believe that they had ever belonged to one another.

The children were reminded of hens in a farmyard, as they watched the scarecrows. One of them would seize a wisp of straw and carry it into a corner, while all the others would pursue him, and try to snatch the trophy away.

The little three-legged scarecrow had given up all attempt to walk, and was simply rolling along the ground. 'Who has won?' she asked, as her face appeared uppermost for an instant.

'The Bogles have won,' said Gummidge. 'And the Swedes have lost everything.'

He looked proudly about him, and then stooped over something limp that was lying on the ground.

The tallest scarecrow bent down to look. 'That'll be Hannah!' he said. 'She does look in a bad way, poor thing.'

Chapter 16

All the other scarecrows crowded round to look at poor Hannah Harrow, who was indeed a sad sight. Even her face had dwindled and her body was as flat as an unstuffed pin-cushion. Occasionally she gave a little gusty sigh.

'You great, gaping, gawky softs,' said an excited voice. The children looked round, and saw that Earthy Mangold was standing just behind them.

'Why don't you *do* something?' she enquired.

'Ooh aye, my dear,' said Gummidge hurriedly,

and picking up Hannah Harrow by the head, he dangled her about until a perfect torrent of sawdust rained from her body.

'She'll trickle to death, if you do that,' screamed Earthy Mangold, who seized Hannah and laid her on the ground again. Then she began to stuff handfuls of sawdust into the sick scarecrow's side. All the time she stuffed, she made consoling noises.

'There, there, my dearie!' she said. 'You'll soon be all right again now.'

'It'll spill out again as soon as you set her on her feet,' remarked Gummidge gloomily.

Earthy Mangold stood up and pulled at a safety pin that was stuck into the tallest scarecrow's shirt. Then she knelt down again, and pinned up the hole.

Hannah Harrow opened her mouth once or twice, but no words came until Earthy had shaken her into shape and run some of the sawdust from out of one leg into the other one.

'I've always been troubled with the mice,' said Hannah. 'I feel all upset, I do.'

'We'll get someone to carry you home,' said Earthy. 'Boggy and Clarty live in the field next-door to you, don't they? They'll help you home.'

'That we won't,' said Clarty. He was a

particularly stiff-looking scarecrow, and he spoke in a husky voice.

'We won't take her, not if she's got the mice, we won't. We might catch 'em.'

He moved away, and began to hurry across the field. A great many of the other scarecrows followed his example. The children heard them muttering, 'We don't want the mice. She'll give us the mice if we stay here. She ought to be kept separate. I knew a Bogle who died of the mice.'

Soon only two scarecrows were left besides Earthy Mangold, Worzel Gummidge, and Hannah Harrow. These two were elderly lady scarecrows. Susan heard one of them say, 'Didn't you ever hear tell of my Aunt Scarey? She had mice in the head. It wasn't to be wondered at, for she were stuffed with newly-threshed straw and some of the grain was in it.'

'You don't say!' exclaimed the other. 'I reckon we'd best be moving.'

They hobbled away, and still continued to talk of the dreaded mice. Susan heard snatches of their conversation as they went: 'They do say the only cure is to swallow a mouse-trap.'

'I'd sooner be restuffed myself.'

'What a lot they are,' exclaimed Earthy indignantly. 'And now what are we to do with Hannah?'

'We might put her in Gummidge's nest,' suggested Susan.

'The very thing!' cried Earthy, though Gummidge looked a little sulky and said that he hoped Hannah wouldn't meddle with the eggs.

'Of course she won't,' said Earthy.

So John and Susan helped the two scarecrows to carry Hannah into the spinney. They had some difficulty in hauling her into the tree. Gummidge insisted on going first, though he was a shockingly bad climber. The children heard him scuffling about in the nest.

'The cardboard egg's addled,' he said, throwing a handful of sticky pulp down to the ground. 'And the other eggs are cold.'

'What a pity,' cried Susan.

'Well, I don't know about that,' he said. 'Earthy and me don't want to be bothered with sitting. We're going to see a bit of life. I've had a hatch of robins and that and a new wife is enough for one season.'

He hurled the eggs out of the nest.

'I feel that reckless,' he muttered. 'I feel that reckless, I don't care what I do.'

Susan didn't feel reckless. She felt very sad. She was so dreadfully afraid that Worzel Gummidge would leave Scatterbrook and never return again.

She helped Earthy to settle Hannah in the nest,

while Gummidge continued to drop boxes and paper-bags over the side of it.

'Now you'll be all right, my dear, won't you?' asked Earthy.

'Ask her and Gummidge to come back,' whispered Susan to Hannah.

The sick scarecrow held out a dusty arm.

'You'll come back in the morning, won't you?' she asked.

'Ooh aye!' promised Gummidge, and he slid stiffly down the tree trunk.

When the children reached the ground again, they saw that Gummidge and Earthy were holding hands.

'I think we'd better go back to bed,' said John.

'Earthy and me are going for a nice long walk,' said Gummidge.

The children noticed that he was wearing his coat again, and that Mr Robin was nestled contentedly under one ear.

'It's been a lovely day,' went on Gummidge contentedly. 'And the battle was a treat and I've got a beautiful wife.'

'I suppose we'd better go home now,' said Susan.

'Don't let's,' objected John, but his sister saw that Worzel Gummidge did not look as though he wanted to be bothered with any more talk. Indeed, he told them so.

'Ooh aye! You'd best be getting along. I shan't have time to look after you now that I've got a wife of my own.'

'Look after us, indeed!' said John.

Susan pulled him away. She was feeling rather sad and lonely, and she was afraid that Gummidge and his new wife might not stay in Scatterbrook.

Not that it matters, she thought. He says he doesn't want us now.

Perhaps the droop of her head told Gummidge that he had not been very kind, for presently he called out, 'You can come and give us a lift with Hannah in the morning. Goodnight!'

'Goodnight!' said Susan.

'Goodnight!' said John.

'Goodnight!' called Earthy Mangold in her shrill little voice.

Then Susan and John hurried through the copse and along the winding lane that led to the farm.

'We'd better take our boots off,' whispered John as they waited in the porch.

Before they could even begin to unfasten bootlaces, the door was opened from inside.

'Where have you been to?' asked Mrs Braithewaite in an angry voice.

Mrs Braithewaite looked very large and fierce. She appeared to be wearing a row of white rosettes on her forehead, but when the children looked again, they saw that these were only tightly-twisted curling papers.

Emily Goodenough stood by the kitchen door; the candle she held in her hand threw flickering shadows on to the wall.

'Where have you been?' repeated Mrs Braithewaite.

'We've been out,' said John.

'Of all the naughty tricks—' Mrs Braithewaite paused as though she were trying to remember enough cross words to scold them with.

'We haven't been a bit naughty,' protested Susan, but as she spoke Mrs Braithewaite's furious face made her feel naughtier and naughtier and naughtier. Some people always made her feel naughty, however good she might have been.

'Emily said we might go,' muttered John. 'Didn't you, Emily?'

'I never did.'

'Oh, yes,' said Susan. 'You said, "Go where you like and when you like only don't bother me"!'

Emily opened her mouth and then shut it again as she remembered that she *had* said something of the sort, earlier in the afternoon.

'And what have you been doing?' rapped out Mrs Braithewaite, and her curl-papers bobbed fiercely.

'We've been playing with the scarecrows,' whispered Susan, though she didn't expect to be believed.

'You'd best tell the truth now,' warned Mrs Braithewaite.

'Well then, I *will*!' said John defiantly. 'We were asked to go to a scarecrow's birthday party and we went. One of the scarecrows is a very great friend of ours and he's going to be married.'

John felt there was no need to keep Gummidge a secret any longer.

Mrs Braithewaite made a most irritating, clicking noise with her tongue, and then, turning to Emily, she said, 'I've never come across such badly behaved and brought-up children in all my born days!'

Now, it so happened that Emily had not been getting on very well with her sister that evening, and it happened, too, that she could not bear other people to find fault with the children. After all, Emily had been their nurse and she had helped to bring them up.

'You said we might go,' said Susan pleadingly.

'I dare say I did,' said Emily. 'But I didn't

understand what you wanted to do. Now come along to bed, my dearies.'

Mrs Braithewaite clicked her tongue once more.

'Have you or anyone else ever heard of scarecrows giving birthday parties?' she demanded. 'Answer me that, Emily. I should have thought you'd been ashamed to listen to the children telling a pack of lies.'

'They've always been fanciful,' said Emily. Susan longed to hug her, but Mrs Braithewaite stood between them.

'Fanciful!' snorted the farmer's wife. 'If I'd anything to do with them I'd make them give a straightforward explanation of their goings-on.'

'You've not got anything to do with them,' snapped Emily. 'And a cold will be the explanation if they don't get off to bed as quickly as knife!'

The children were thankful enough for Emily's roughness as she whisked them out of their clothes and hustled them into their beds. Her hands felt chillier and bonier than ever, but she did not ask questions, and talked comfortingly about hot-water bottles.

'It's all my fault,' declared Emily at last. 'I ought to have taken better notice of what you were saying. Now you'd best go to sleep as soon as may be or you won't be able to enjoy your last day in Scatterbrook.'

'Last day?' repeated Susan.

'Had you forgotten that?' asked Emily. 'Today's Tuesday, you know. It is morning already because the clock's struck twelve, and you go home on Wednesday.'

'Oh dear!' sighed Susan.

Somehow the children had lost count of the days in Scatterbrook. It seemed such a long time now since the end of whooping-cough and the beginning of Gummidge.

All the same, thought Susan, as she scrambled into bed. All the same, perhaps it's a good thing we are going. I don't know what we should do if Worzel Gummidge went first.

Chapter 17

Breakfast next morning was rather a gloomy meal. Mrs Braithewaite was still cross. She slopped coffee into all the saucers, hacked great hunks of bread off the loaf, and made clicking noises with her tongue the whole time.

Before the meal was over, Farmer Braithewaite stumped into the kitchen. He carried something over his shoulder—something that looked like a half-filled sack with a knobble at one end and two sticks at the other. This he flung down into a corner of the room, and then turned and scowled at the children.

John looked with interest at the writing bundle in the corner. Susan looked at it too, but she felt so worried she did not dare to speak. She was terribly afraid that the sack was not really a sack at all.

'You might keep your rubbish out of my nice clean kitchen,' snapped Mrs Braithewaite.

Then because John was a particularly cheerful little boy and not easily depressed even by Mrs Braithewaite's crossness, he asked, 'Are there any ferrets in that bag, Mr Braithewaite?'

'Ferrets!' said the farmer. 'Ferrets, indeed!'

Susan hardly noticed his anger; she was so interested in the sack, which continued to wriggle feebly. It was—and yet it couldn't be—and yet it was—Hannah Harrow! Susan recognized her by the safety pin in her side. She pushed back her chair.

'Hey! Keep still!' thundered the farmer. Susan obeyed him, and so did Hannah Harrow, who stopped still in the very middle of a quiver.

The farmer turned to his wife, and said, 'I've just come back from Ten-acre, and what do you think I saw there?'

'Click! Click!' went Mrs Braithewaite's tongue.

'My new scarecrow has been pulled to pieces. There are bits of it scattered all over the plough. There are footmarks too—small footmarks—and the seeds are trampled, and there are the marks of other things that look like crutches or stilts.'

Mrs Braithewaite looked sourly at the children.

'You'd best ask those two about the footmarks,' she said.

'I don't need to ask,' retorted the farmer. 'I remember what you told me this morning. But that's not all. I went into the spinney and saw a lot of rubbish lying under an oak tree; there were china eggs and bits of chocolate and all kinds of litter. And hanging across a branch of the oak tree I saw that old scarecrow.' He pointed to Hannah Harrow, who still sagged in a corner of the room.

'Now, I happen to know that that scarecrow belongs to Mr Needham of Penfold. How did it get into my tree? That's what I want to know.'

'You'd better ask the children,' repeated Mrs Braithewaite.

'You needn't tell me that the children carried Mr Needham's scarecrow all the way from Penfold,' snapped the farmer.

'We didn't,' cried John and Susan together. They were glad to be able to say something that could be understood.

'Did you put her into the oak tree?' asked the farmer.

'We helped to,' said Susan. She wouldn't have answered at all if she had not seen Hannah

Harrow moving again; but she wanted to prevent Farmer Braithewaite from noticing.

'Who did you help?' he enquired.

'We helped two of the other scarecrows,' said Susan. And then, seeing the farmer open his mouth angrily, she sobbed, 'I know it sounds silly, but we really truly did! The field was full of scarecrows last night. They were angry with the one you put up, and so they had a battle and fought against him.' She choked, and stopped speaking.

'Don't you remember what that old scarecrow maker said?' asked John suddenly. 'He said you would be sorry if you made your own scarecrows.'

'So that old good-for-nothing is at the bottom of it, is he?' said Mr Braithewaite. 'Was he in the fields last night!'

'No, he wasn't,' said John. 'At least if he was, we didn't see him.'

'I don't know what to make of it all,' said the farmer.

'There's nothing to make of it,' said Mrs Braithewaite. 'You don't know how much harm a pair of destructive children can do; that's all there is about it.'

'We aren't destructive,' said John angrily. 'You've no right to say that. We haven't done any harm at all.'

The farmer shook his head again. 'I don't know what to make of it,' he repeated. 'I'm sick of scarecrows; they're nothing but trouble. A queer thing happened yesterday morning in Ten-acre. The rooks was all collected round the scarecrow I'd just set up. I've never seen a thing like that happen before. You needn't tell me that the children had tamed all the wild rooks!'

'You never know what children will be up to,' said Mrs Braithewaite glumly.

'Well, anyway I'm going to buy one of those new windmill scarers that I saw in Penfold.'

'Why don't you use that one?' asked Mrs Braithewaite, and she pointed towards Hannah Harrow.

'Because, I tell you, I'm sick of scarecrows!' He turned his head as footsteps sounded outside the kitchen door. 'Hi, Bill!' he shouted. 'You take this old scarecrow out of the kitchen and burn it on the rubbish heap. I'm going to Penfold this morning.'

Bill, the ploughman, stumped into the kitchen.

'Oh! please,' pleaded Susan.

'Please don't!' said John. 'I'll give you all the money I have. I'd like to buy Hannah—I mean the scarecrow.'

Chapter 18

The farmer followed Bill out of the kitchen, and Susan put her head down on the table and sobbed bitterly.

'Now don't take on, dearie,' said Mrs Braithewaite, who never could bear the sight of tears. 'We all know children will be children.'

'Scarecrows will be scarecrows, too,' said John boldly. Mrs Braithewaite frowned at him, and said, 'Now don't talk silly. We'll let bygones be bygones. It's no use fretting. You go up to your rooms and have a nice lie down. You must be worn out with traipesing over the fields last night.'

'Can't we go for a walk?' sobbed Susan, who still hoped to rescue poor Hannah Harrow.

'That you can't,' said Mrs Braithewaite. 'Why, you haven't got a pair of boots fit to wear. They are all muddied up.'

The children saw that it was no use to argue. Besides, they really did feel terribly sleepy.

'What about Hannah?' whispered Susan, as they reached the top of the stairs.

'Bill will have gone to the fields by now,' said John. 'He never makes bonfires in the morning.'

Then the children went to their own rooms and rested. Emily tiptoed into their rooms at dinner-time, but Susan and John were sleeping so soundly that she had not the heart to disturb them.

At three o'clock Susan opened her eyes. Then she sniffed once or twice; the room was full of the smell of smoke. She ran across to the window and looked down into the yard. Bill, the ploughman, had just set light to a bonfire, which he was stirring with a pitchfork. By the side of it, and looking rather thinner than before, lay Hannah Harrow.

Susan rushed to the bedroom door and turned the handle. Whatever happened, she felt she must go down and save the little scarecrow. She tugged furiously at the door but it would not open. Somebody had turned the key in the lock. She darted back to the window, and looked out again. Bill was swinging Hannah Harrow by the head!

'Don't!' screamed Susan, and she hammered on the window. Bill was startled by her voice and he looked all round the yard. Hannah's sacking skirt was trailing in the mud and poor Hannah's sawdust was fast trickling away.

'Don't!' shouted Susan. Then she heard John crying, 'Don't!' too.

Poor Bill, who could not imagine where the voices came from, turned round and round in bewilderment. Then, still grasping Hannah's head, he stepped towards the blazing bonfire. But before he could swing back his arm to throw the unfortunate little scarecrow, someone very large and fierce-looking stumped into the yard.

'Gummidge!' shouted Susan delightedly.

Gummidge waved his arms and advanced towards the terrified ploughman. Then he raised a knobbly fist and hit Bill hard in the face, and snatched Hannah from him.

Bill staggered and fell over his pitchfork. Then he rolled a little way. By the time he had stood up again, and had rubbed his eyes which were quite blinded by smoke, Gummidge had disappeared from his sight. But Susan, who could see over the wall, caught a glimpse of Gummidge and Earthy Mangold as they disappeared down the lane. Between them they carried Hannah Harrow. Her head was sagging sideways, but Susan noticed that she was smiling feebly. Then the door handle rattled, and Emily cried.

'Why, whatever have you been and locked your door for?'

'I didn't,' shouted Susan. 'It's locked from outside. I've been trying to get out.'

'So that's why you've been making such a noise,' said Emily, and she turned the key and opened the door.

'Come to think of it,' she said. 'I must have locked the door myself. I tiptoed in a little while back, but you were sleeping so soundly I didn't like to wake you.'

John's voice sounded from the next door room—

'Hi! I'm locked in! I want to get out.'

'All right,' called Emily. 'I'm coming. Don't rattle the door to pieces. I never knew such a boy.' As she was going out of the room, she turned to Susan. 'I can't think what's coming over me,' she said. 'But I've got into a habit of locking doors lately. It's ever since the handle came off the larder door. You have to lock that if you want to keep the cat out.'

She scuttled away, leaving Susan to go down to the kitchen, where John joined her.

They were not able to ask each other any questions, because Bill, the ploughman, was describing his adventure to Emily Goodenough and Mrs Braithewaite. He was saying, in a high voice, 'And just as I was going to throw the scarecrow on the bonfire, a great lout of a man jumped out at me, and knocked me silly. I lay on the ground for an hour or more—'

'Oh!' whispered Susan. '*What* a story!'

'And when I came to,' continued Bill. 'When I came to, the other chap had gone and so had the scarecrow.'

'Maybe you threw it on to the fire as you fell,' suggested Emily Goodenough.

'Mebbe I did,' agreed Bill. 'My trousers were singed and my eyes were full of smoke, so I couldn't rightly see. I reckon that is what happened. I don't see why anyone should want to steal a scarecrow.'

'What did the other chap look like?' asked Emily.

'He was a great fierce sort of fellow. He looked like—' Here Bill stopped speaking and scratched his head. 'I know he put me in mind of someone. He looked for all the world like our old scarecrow from out of Ten-acre Field.'

'Well, I never did!' exclaimed Mrs Braithewaite as she wiped the flour from her arms. 'I should have thought we'd have finished with scarecrows by now. The master's just setting up a new-fangled windmill scarer in Ten-acre.'

'Well let's have tea now,' said Emily. 'I've all the packing to do afterwards. What about those scones you were baking?'

Mrs Braithewaite went to the oven, and pulled out a tin full of the soda scones she made so beautifully.

The last tea was quite a feast. There was a new cake, and a jar of apple-jelly, scones and queen-cakes and brandy-snaps. The farmer had recovered his temper. John and Susan were quite happy again now that they knew Hannah Harrow was safe and Emily was in her very best mood.

Mrs Braithewaite actually seemed sorry that they were going away, and even the farmer muttered that the place would be lost without them. It is strange how the grumpiest people turn pleasant when it is time to say goodbye.

John and Susan felt partly glad and partly sorry. It would be exciting to go home again, to see their mother and father, the house dog, the house cat, and the canary. It would be lovely to sit once more in the fussy little train that puffed so slowly along the valley. It would be fun to rush into their own schoolroom and see if anything new had arrived in the house. All that would be lovely. But it was rather sad to think they could not see Scatterbrook again until the summer, when the hay would have made the hedges look quite short and stumpy, and when days would begin early and last till ten o'clock. Neither of them wanted to think much about Scatterbrook in the summer, for where would Worzel Gummidge be?

After tea, when Emily went upstairs to pack, John and Susan followed the farmer out into the yard. They went to say goodbye to all the animals, to the cows and horses and hens and chickens. They stayed rather a long time with the old black sow, because they felt they had seen so little of her that they ought to make the most of the time.

They had so many things to do that they did not remember Gummidge again until late that evening as they sat over the kitchen fire drinking bread and milk, and roasting their faces in the firelight.

Emily was finishing the packing, and the farmer and his wife were drowsing on either side of the fender.

Susan was reminded of the queer evening she had spent alone in the kitchen on the night when Worzel Gummidge had paid his first visit.

'I wonder when we shall see him again?' she whispered, and as she spoke, she heard the sound of creaky footsteps on the flags outside.

'Look!' said John, and he pointed to the window-blind. There was a queer raggedy shadow on it—the shadow of a head in a strangely-shaped hat. Perched on top of it was something that might have been a rosette. Susan knew it was the tiny fluffed-up body of Father Robin.

A little tinkle sounded in the hearth, as Mrs Braithewaite dropped a knitting-pin. She was asleep and so was the farmer.

John and Susan did not dare to stir.

The blind became a blank again, and once more they heard the sound of footsteps, nearer to the door this time. The latch rattled, the door opened, and the farmer stirred in his sleep.

Gummidge's face appeared in the doorway. He stepped into the kitchen.

'Evenin'!' he wheezed. 'I've come to say goodbye. I'm leavin' Scatterbrook.'

The farmer jerked his head, and opened his eyes.

'Why!' he began, but even as he spoke the door was shut.

'I thought I saw a scarecrow looking at me,' he mumbled. His remark awakened Mrs Braithewaite.

'You've scarecrows on the brain!' she said.

Suddenly Father Robin fluttered across the room.

'How did that bird get here?' The farmer sounded puzzled.

'The wind must have blown the door ajar,' said his wife. 'Unless the children—' But, before she could finish her sentence, Susan rushed over to the window and caught Father Robin as he beat himself against the panes. His soft brown body quivered in her hand for a moment, and then he settled down into the hollow of her palm.

'I do believe he knows me,' she said.

'Let me hold him,' begged John.

'Best put him out before the cat comes in,' said Mrs Braithewaite, and John opened the door.

The robin flew out of Susan's hand, and zigzagged away across the moonlit yard.

The children thought that they saw two rather lumpy and raggedy figures walking through the yard gateway, but they couldn't be quite sure, for—

'Come in,' said Mrs Braithewaite. 'Come in, and shut the door.'

That visit was the last one Worzel Gummidge paid to the farm, but the children saw him again when they had left Scatterbrook some miles behind them.

The fussy little train which had been puffing like a green dragon between the woods and fields, suddenly came to a stop in a siding. It waited for so long that the children lowered the window, and put their heads out.

'Look!' cried Susan. She shouted so loudly that the elderly lady, who had promised to look after the children on their journey to London, dropped her book and little handbag. It was really rather lucky, because the bag opened, and all sorts of oddments went rolling over the carriage floor. The elderly lady was so busy picking them up that she didn't notice what the children were doing.

'Look! Look! Look!' yelled Susan, and she pointed to a small wedge-shaped field. In the middle of it, standing side by side, their clothes flapping busily in the wind, stood Worzel Gummidge and Earthy Mangold.

John nearly tumbled out of the window as he leaned forward to look.

Gummidge's face was as knobbly as ever: his hat was battered, his clothes were shabby, but he beamed happily at Earthy Mangold.

A few yards behind them stood Hannah Harrow. She was still thin, and she still sagged a little at the waist, but she too looked happy.

Earthy Mangold raised her funny little face,

and smiled at the children as they waved their handkerchiefs.

For a moment they were afraid that Gummidge would not see them. Then he raised a stiff arm, and lifted his hat. A small brown thing whirled away from the brim, and flew to the topmost branch of a silver birch sapling.

Gummidge began to stump slowly towards the fence that bordered the railway siding.

'Gummidge!' yelled John.

'Darling Gummidge,' cried Susan. 'We're going home to London.'

'Me and her's staying here for a bit,' wheezed Gummidge, and he pointed to Earthy, who was hurrying towards the fence. 'Ooh aye, we see a bit of life here, and the trains is company.'

'How's Hannah?' asked John.

'Not so bad as she were. She's staying along of us as maid-of-all-work.'

The train began to move slowly out of the siding.

'When shall we see you again?' yelled Susan.

'*She's* a fancy for Lunnon,' shouted Gummidge. 'She's daft to see the shops.'

The train began to move more quickly.

'Come and see us soon!' begged John.

'Ooh aye!' came the reply.

As the train steamed away, the children leaned

out of the window. Gummidge and Earthy continued to wave until a corner of the railway bank hid them from sight.

'After all,' said Susan contentedly. 'After all, it would have been horrid to stay in Scatterbrook after Gummidge had left.'

'And horrider to leave Scatterbrook if Gummidge was still there,' added John. 'Besides, he says he'll come to London.'

The elderly lady crossed over to their side of the carriage, and pulled up the window.